BOBBY MEHDWAN

Blue Panther

60S

First edition

ISBN: 978-1-7398131-7-8

Editing by Anne Brewer

*This book was professionally typeset on Reedsy.
Find out more at reedsy.com*

For Nisha, Serena and Amar
For Liberty

Contents

GET LIBERTY ONE

Read the follow on after *Blue Panther*.

Get it at 60strategies.com/Liberty_One

BLUE PANTHER

BOBBY MEHDWAN

Glossary

- ABLE DOG: US Navy Douglas or A-1 (AD) Skyraider
- CQ: Carrier Qualification
- CPO: Chief Petty Officer
- GI: Government Issue (WW2 soldiers)
- GPA: Grade Point Average
- ICBM: Intercontinental Ballistic Missile
- LSO: Landing Signal Officer
- MiG: Mikoyan and Gurevich
- MLR: Main Line of Resistance
- NAS: Naval Air Station
- NASA: National Aeronautics and Space Administration
- PoW: Prisoner of War
- RUSTY BUCKET: USS Valley Forge (CV-45)
- SAM: Surface to Air Missile
- SNJ: North American Aircraft Company, WW2 Trainer Aircraft
- TNT: Trinitrotoluene (an explosive)
- U2: Reconnaissance Aircraft
- UN: United Nations
- USC: The University of Southern California
- XO: Executive Officer

About

A fictional story inspired by real events, people and places.

* * *

Characters speak and act according to the attitudes of their time and setting.

* * *

Scroll to the back of the book to leave a review and join the newsletter to get free goodies.

* * *

Written in American English.

CHAPTER 1 - INSOLENT DAYS

Late-March 1950, Texas, Sunday Morning

The red, stacked-wing crop duster made a satisfying, throaty growl, ducking and diving through the tall trees, barely twenty feet above the hedges of suburban Texas. It felt like summer had arrived early, with the day already cooking at ninety degrees.

Eighteen-year-old Jim Cobb, goggle-eyed and nestled in the cocoon of the back seat, felt like he was in his very own fighter plane charging into battle. Dropping as low as he dared, he felt mesmerized as house after house whizzed by on his right.

He caught a glimpse of several large balsa planes, dangling from the ceiling just inside his bedroom window, as he flew past his own white GI home.

With a gentle push on the throttle, he lowered his head and egged on the plane towards its target which lay straight ahead.

Mrs. Susan Cobb, baking in the kitchen of the white house, stopped to listen as the sound of the engine grew from nothing to a deafening roar. She froze, holding her breath, eyes wide, fingers still curled in a bowl of sticky dough, and turned to the window. Her retinas caught an unlikely streak of scarlet shooting over the hedges, but the noise faded as soon as she ran

1

to the window. Whatever it was, it had disappeared like a flash of lightning over the neighboring yards.

She stood with glazed eyes, her hands still covered in ginger-bread, trying to make sense of it all. She blinked and refocused, though she still saw the unlikely imprint of a biplane the size of a small boat hovering low above the trees.

"Jim!" she screamed, cursing under her breath and shaking the dough from her fingers as if she were about to step into a ring with the young man.

The plane was already on its approach to number fifty-six, less than a mile from Jim's house. He pulled on the stick and winced as it whizzed over a last clump of trees, almost close enough to strip the leaves from the treetops. The plane sped over another yard, jolting a young woman from her slumber on a sunbed.

She looked up with a start and dropped her still open glossy. A bottle of sunscreen spilled on the ground as she sprang to her feet and turned toward a stiff roll of paper that had fallen in the yard ten feet away.

Jim thanked the heavens that the paper roll hadn't hit her. He yelled, "Happy Birthday, JoAnn!" imagining that she could hear him over the sound of the pistons.

He began a steep climb, pushing the plane for all it was worth toward small wisps of cloud in the clear blue sky by the time JoAnn had grabbed the package.

She hastily wrapped a towel around herself and looked up at him. Then she unpacked the broadsheet roll to reveal a curled up birthday card inside, picturing an animated lady in a yellow and red striped dress holding a birthday cake on a handheld stand. For Jim, it was the safest option he could find easily without walking on thin ice; he didn't yet know her nearly as well as he

2

wished.

He'd already leveled off and turned north again. "Yoo-hoo, JoAnn! What did you think of that?" he yelled, looking down and punching the air in triumph. He was besotted. JoAnn looked glorious, even from hundreds of feet up.

She was ecstatic, jumping up and down and waving the card madly at him.

Jim tore off his cap and swung it in the jet stream, almost dropping it. "See, Daddy? That's my girl!" he shouted into the air.

He straightened the plane and enjoyed a few moments over Boar Creek in rural South Texas before his thoughts turned to home. With one arm pointing straight ahead, he led the charge back to the farm where the plane lived.

His smile disappeared when he heard the engine sputter. He looked down at the instruments and flipped a bank of switches to make sure he hadn't forgotten anything. With dawning horror, his heart skipped a beat when he saw the fuel gauge sitting on empty. He tapped it with a knuckle, but it remained lifeless. "Damn it," he cursed with a glance at his watch. He'd lost track of time, completely caught up in his mission.

He'd hatched the plan the week before. Bruno, a high school football ace, had made an impression on JoAnn. She'd driven to school in his father's fancy new fiery-red Bel Air, and now Jim had a battle on his hands to get her attention back. He had planned to show her the world from the airplane on her birthday, thinking Bruno would look very small from the clouds.

But he could only count one dollar and thirteen cents, which he'd earned, working a few evenings and weekends a month at various jobs on the farm, repairing and cleaning machines under Farmer Lebbe's tutelage. That wouldn't buy a tank of gas.

A third? No. A tenth? Maybe, just. Thirty minutes of flying, if that, and no fancy moves. He'd be counting every second. But he couldn't risk JoAnn's life. Besides, he had to help Mama with the weekly shopping while his father was away.

He would clean a couple of tractors and a Massey in exchange for gas, or take her to a game instead—though that ass, Bruno, would be playing for sure. She'd probably just go in his fancy car. The game didn't seem like an option.

He went straight to Lebbe when Bruno gave her another ride to school the next morning. He offered to fly the plane over the edge of a small field to test the replacement duster box. He added that he needed his annual license hours and would do all the cleaning if he could just borrow the plane with a tank of fuel. The farmer said the gas supply was backed up and the plane was almost dry. It would be an hour in the air at most.

That left no room for an extra body. Jim would have to go it alone and deliver a Sunday surprise to JoAnn instead. He told her he would, "drop by." Intrigued, she replied that she'd be home.

The engine now coughed as if it had caught a bug. He tried the switches again, but nothing happened. He couldn't land on the houses below. All the open fields and empty roads surrounding the farm were still ten miles away, though just visible straight ahead. An open farm or long road might do, but it would cost dearly to retrieve the empty plane. It might never get out again.

The gas-starved engine sputtered on, and the plane fell as fast as Jim's hubris. With five miles to go, the roads were full of traffic. He circled a small field but changed course for a divided highway straight ahead. The cars would have to part like the Red Sea.

The engine shut down, leaving the plane in a smooth, steep

glide a hundred feet in the air. He aimed for the highway and pulled the stick, but the wings had no lift. He swerved into a clump of East Texas pines in front of a large house. The wheels clipped the tallest tree, then bounced off a sloping roof.

He fought the switches again, but his hand hit the duster handle, releasing white gunk that splattered on a black Buick Special still wet from a car wash below. He recoiled back into his cockpit as the owner—about to polish the shiny hood—looked up and cursed the sky.

"Get out of the way! Out of the way!" he yelled, dropping the plane onto the busy road. The tires hit a clear stretch of pavement with a bone-crunching thud, then bounced and wobbled in the air before landing in a plume of smoke.

Vehicles screeched behind him as the plane rolled on. An older driver just ahead hadn't seen him in his rear view.

"Move! Get out of the way! Move!"

The plane threatened to plow into the car as oncoming vehicles screeched to a halt.

The horrified elderly driver glanced in the mirror and slammed on the pedal just before the plane quietly crawled to a stop in front of a gas station.

An eerie, disbelieving silence filled the air. The clouds of dust settled. Shell-shocked drivers emerged from their cars to see the spectacle. The gas man froze, still pumping a tank.

Jim got out, took off his goggles, and walked towards him sheepishly. "Could you, uh, fill her up, please?"

He fumbled inside his pockets, but all he could produce were a few quarters.

There was no fuel for an airplane, so later that day, Farmer Lebbe, with Jim's help, wheeled it to the edge of the gas station.

Every passing motorist slowed to admire it as if it were a new landmark.

Jim looked worried and remorseful when he was driven home in the farmer's rusty old pickup.

"Jim, the station has no need for avgas. So, I'll have to come back with one or two cans, and ask them to close the road so we can get it back in the air."

The farmer pulled out of the station and onto the highway as cars with rubberneckers drove by. "I don't know how long it's going to take. It's a good thing there's a long stretch here," he said.

Jim was quiet.

"Are you sure you're alright now?" the farmer asked.

Jim felt ashamed and nodded, though he couldn't think of an answer. He was sure that Lebbe was angry inside. Fortunately, he was a gentle, even-tempered Steady Eddie who hadn't exploded in his face. Jim didn't want to provoke any anger.

Instead, he made another feeble apology and said, "Someday, all these cars will be flying." It was a dumb thing to say, though he was sure it would happen.

The farmer looked lost for words, then said with a thin smile, "Yeah, maybe. But not in my lifetime." He continued. "You know, you're lucky you didn't have a serious accident."

Jim's face fell. It was a huge understatement, and he would be hearing those words over and over like a stuck gramophone.

"I won't tell," the farmer said with a reassuring smile.

Jim knew it was impossible to keep a secret like that across the state, let alone in Boar Creek.

Twenty minutes later, Farmer Lebbe turned off Mona Lisa on the radio and pulled up to the gate of Jim's house. A short, sloping path cut through the lawn surrounding the house and led to the front door. It was clad in white and had vertical panels with pale blue soffits. The front had a small porch, its ceiling held up by wooden pillars. Jim's room was at the back, where he'd last been seen flying.

He noticed that Lebbe had broken into a sweat the moment his mama's aproned figure appeared outside. He got out of the car and nodded to the farmer, but received only a strained smile in return. Lebbe glanced at Susan and drove away in a hurry, as if fleeing an impending typhoon. She glared after him as the car disappeared and the dust settled.

Susan trained her sights on Jim like a rocket launcher and hurried down the path to meet him. "I've been worried about you," she said.

His first thought, standing next to her, was that he looked like he had come to the wrong house, like he belonged to a different family. Slim, sturdy, and quite tall, he could have spent the day herding cattle—his hair disheveled from being outdoors, and his face oil-stained from inspecting the plane and other farm machinery. Susan, on the other hand, was small in stature, and her clothes were neat and tidy. She had always looked like someone with wisdom and determination.

"Come inside now. And eat your dinner before it gets cold." It was an order. "Then go and finish your chores, please."

She walked back up the path, stopped halfway and turned. Her scowl returned and Jim blushed, but something else had caught her eye over his shoulder. She stood up straight to the full extent of her small height with her hands on her hips. Jim turned to see Mr. Wilman peering furtively from behind his netted windows across the street. No one missed a movement with that man around.

He rushed into the house with his mama. In predictable

7

fashion, she closed the door and implored him to act his age and be more considerate of others. She wagged her finger in the direction of the yard and said she had seen the red plane, which, "had no reason to be there."

Jim, also true to form, lamented a lack of understanding. "They make those planes to fly low, Mama. That's why it's a crop duster. To spray the crops. You can't do that from up high," he pleaded, thinking he was being honest and resourceful.

Looking lost for words at first, she said, "Do you see any crops in that yard over there, Jim? Anything that needs spraying? Or the next one? How about that one over there?"

She wasn't expecting an answer, but he lost his tongue anyway.

Susan leaned forward and looked him in the eye. "I don't want you anywhere near that plane again. Do you hear me?"

The words slapped Jim in the face, even though he had been expecting this moment.

"And you owe poor JoAnn an apology," she said. "June was in the store. You could have knocked the girl out dropping things from the sky."

Jim's eyes suddenly brightened as an image of JoAnn's brown, straight hair, hanging down to her shoulders and parted on the left, swept across his mind and imprinted itself on his imagination, just as the plane had been on Mama's. She didn't need an apology for a birthday to remember. His thoughts flashed back to when he was nine and they'd first played tennis against a wall, and it had surprised him then that he had never actually seen a girl play the game.

"Jim? Did you hear what I just said?"

His face relaxed and a reminiscent smile appeared.

Her eyes rolled. "And what's so amusing?"

"JoAnn, Mama, you should have seen her face. I can still see it now. It must have sounded like a freight train passing through her yard!"

Susan was speechless as he disappeared into the kitchen and wolfed down his dinner. Then, he went out back to tend to the small chicken coop in their meager barn.

CHAPTER 2 - PLANES

Same evening

Jim lay on his bed, looking out the window with his arms crossed behind his head, feeling the exhilarating energy of the day still pumping through his veins.

He picked up a framed photo of a fishing trip with his father from the previous year. They looked proud with their rods and a catch in Jim's hand. Now, Jim hadn't heard from him in two months, when he'd turned eighteen. It seemed strangely out of character. Was the mail lost somewhere over thousands of miles of ocean?

He reached over and picked up a shiny silver Douglas DC-3 lapel badge, which his father had left as a memento of the workhorse he'd flown against the Soviet blockade of Berlin. He was one of the last of the Army Air Corps to return from the war in Europe, though he'd barely stepped inside the front door when they sent him straight back to the Far East to monitor the Communists from bases in Japan. Though Jim had barely seen the man through his teens, he knew he hoped Jim would be a pilot, just like himself and Jim's grandfather. He had said God made the Cobbs for the air.

Jim lay back on his bed, wondering how he was going to fight his mama over his grounding, knowing that he had to be back in the sky. His thoughts returned to his first ride in the back of the two-seater crop duster with Lebbe at the age of fourteen. He mastered holding the plane steady in a crosswind on a spraying run and learned to pull the stick back on takeoff by fifteen. He could keep the plane level in a cruise and quickly grasped how to turn with the tailplane and rudder and stay level in a side wind.

His father returned home from demobilization just as Jim turned sixteen. He got a student pilot's certificate and a stack of books for his birthday and they jumped right back into the plane together. Lebbe made them pay for gas and insurance, but it was as cheap as a bus fare. Susan was scared to death, but Jim knew this was it—approaching and landing the plane on a grass strip was the most fun he'd ever had. His father gave him confidence, but he was demanding and uncompromising about safety, reminding him twice, with obvious discomfort, that he could get killed if he did not take great care at all times. Jim soloed a few months later after an intense forty-five hours in the air and about the same time reading books and plotting courses.

In the middle of the year, his father went to Berlin and stayed for almost twelve months. With Lebbe's help, Jim maintained his proficiency and checked out with a qualified instructor the following June when his father returned briefly for a second time. Jim was seventeen when he received his pilot's certificate under his father's watchful eye. The man left for Japan at the end of that summer, saying that the Communists were angling for trouble right where the Nazis had left off. But he hadn't revealed what he was doing nor when he'd return home. Jim had written that he would fly his mama over so they could be together a little more often.

Now, still holding the photo, he walked to the window. His face relaxed as he imagined flying through the atmosphere, looking at the city lights below. The crickets were chirping, and the sun had painted a fiery red and pale orange sky on the horizon. A few stars had appeared in the deep blue heavens above. He scanned the strip of new suburban GI homes along Williston Loop, which were all for returning military personnel, just like his own. The new construction had brought an infectious optimism and energy. Fancy automation, unimaginable before the war, had appeared in every corner of life.

Ducking back inside, he retrieved a stack of Popular Mechanics from a corner of his room and thumbed through them on the floor, enthralled by the science and technology that promised to revolutionize the future. A life of leisure, abundant free solar energy, jetpacks, interstellar travel, and life on a lunar base would be here by the year 2000, with mankind forever unshackled from Earth, it foretold.

Later that evening, as he sat watching *Space Patrol*, he felt that the crazy future was still too far away. He wanted robots to dress him for bed now, and a bubble car to speed him along the skyway tomorrow. He desperately wished he could express his vision to someone, anyone, but his mama didn't get it, and his father was still away.

Still, with a pencil and pad, he sketched futuristic airplanes and high-altitude supersonic jets, the blueprints of which he'd turned into balsas just a few years back. To his nostrils, the glue had smelled like the future. "One day, Mama," he had promised, with deep and sincere conviction, "I'll make real ones and fly them faster than the speed of sound."

"For passengers, I hope, Jim. Not fighting. We don't need any more conflict in the world," she said. "We've seen enough of

12

that. But I fear we have a fight on our hands to get your father back."

"There will be no more wars in the future, Mama. We'll all be exploring the stars instead. Don't you worry about that."

* * *

The next day

The school year was almost over, and Jim was sitting with Susan at a desk in the principal's office. The man across the table was wearing a light-colored suit over a white shirt and plain tie. Next to him was a guidance counselor in a ruffled blouse and black jacket.

The principal took off his glasses and said confidently, "We received a positive response to Jim's college applications." He looked down and flipped through some papers, then looked up at Susan. "Tarleton State, Arlington, and Texas Tech have all accepted Jim for agricultural science. He's now in a great position to make his first, second, and third choices. May I call you Susan?"

She smiled with obvious relief.

"They're all good, but our recommendation would be Tarleton. It's not too far from home, so you'll get to see him more often," he added with a smile.

Susan beamed back at him. "Yes, that's what we decided."

The principal turned to Jim, though he remained reclined in his chair, his eyes tracking a pair of red kites flying across the sky outside the window.

"Now, Jim, do we have a second or third choice?"

Jim straightened and scanned the headmaster and the counselor.

"Come on now, name your choices," Susan said, encouraging him with a smile.

He shrugged.

She answered the principal for him. "We already talked about this and agree on Tarleton, then Texas Tech—"

"I don't know, Mama." Jim sighed, shifting in his seat.

All eyes turned to him.

"What's the matter?" Susan asked.

Jim hesitated. "I've been thinking, I really want to make or fly airplanes, Mama. You know, like Daddy does, and Grandpa."

Susan considered her next move, straightened her face, and said, "Jim, we went over this."

The counselor sat up straight in her seat.

The principal broke the silence. "Okay, so you're thinking of a future in aircraft design or engineering? Is that what you're saying now?"

Jim sat forward, shrugged, and nodded, though he knew this could not have come at a worse time. "Well, yeah. Something like that."

The counselor said to Susan, "Well, there are lots of opportunities for scientists and engineers. New types of airplanes will fly faster than sound in the future. You'll be on the other side of the world in just a few hours. Is that what you're thinking about, Jim?"

Susan looked at him. "I know you love that plane back at the farm." She turned back to the counselor. "And yes, he's good with his hands." She half-laughed at a thought that popped into her head. "He liked building models out of odd pieces. He probably got that from his father. And he's already fixing machines down at the farm and flying that plane, and still only eighteen. Farmer Lebbe's training him and looking after him. Jim gets a little money."

The counselor scanned her papers. "Okay, why don't we go over the facts again? SAT scores: Science: 580. Math: 575 against an average of 509." She turned the pages and picked out some numbers. "And reading, comprehension, and writing are good: 560 against a 530 average. His GPA is 3.2, but I think he could raise that a little if he paid more attention in some of his last classes." She looked up at Jim to gauge his reaction, then read again. "Art doesn't look like a favorite, although he seems to be good at technical drawings. It does point to something like engineering, but, as you know, applications are already closed for this year. He could try again next year."

"Make a choice now, Jim. It's too late to change course," Susan insisted.

Jim hesitated. "Well, what *about* next year, Mama?"

"What in the world are you going to do for a year?" she asked.

"Sounds like he could get some technical experience on the farm, earn some money, and contribute to his education," the principal said.

"I think I should join the military, Mama."

Susan's face froze then contorted. "What are you saying? Where did all this come from all of a sudden? I thought we had already decided."

Jim didn't answer right away.

"The Air Force?" Susan asked.

"Navy, Mama. So I get to fly the really fast planes all over the world. And it's free. A man came to school to talk about the Holloway Plan." He explained the government's generous offer: it would give him two years of college for free, he'd learn to fly a fighter in Pensacola, followed by three years as a Navy pilot and

15

two as a reservist. He was still mesmerized by the Navy visitor, in all-white uniform with gold wings pinned to his chest, as he explained the opportunity.

Exasperated, Susan turned to the principal. "I want to see his feet on the ground. Making models is one thing, but his father flies planes in the military, and we've hardly seen him in years."

"That would be a seven-year commitment, Jim," said the counselor. "Are you ready for that?"

"They say you can get a thirty-five thousand dollar education for free as a Navy pilot. I saw it at the post office. What could be better than that, Mama? It won't cost a dime."

Susan shifted in her seat. "But Jim, the war's over. We talked about that. The world has changed, and there are other jobs now. What are you going to do in the Navy for seven years? It will just take you away from home, like your father. The last of the men are back from the war. Okay, so your father's not, but it won't be long now," she urged, almost willing it. "They're taking all the good jobs, not going back to the military or anything like that." More confidently, she continued, "Your father says the government is demobilizing, winding down. It's all over, Jim."

She looked up at the principal and the counselor, leaned on the front of her seat, and pleaded, "Doesn't agriculture have engineering? Everything has changed, hasn't it? I hear that technology and machines are going to replace the people. I know that's not a good thing, but Jim could make some of those, couldn't he?"

"Farming? Mama, I just can't—"

"Jim, it will keep you home and safe and in work," she said at once. "You could be a ... an agricultural agent for the county."

Jim felt embarrassed. He couldn't understand her fascination with working on the land or how strongly she still felt about it.

He'd gone along with agricultural science but deeply regretted not taking a stand earlier.

"Look, why don't you talk it over again?" the principal said. "But we have to decide soon and inform the colleges. He could lose his place if he doesn't make a choice in the next few weeks." He looked at Jim. "Maybe you should discuss it with your father?" He looked at Susan. "Is he back soon?"

She sighed, looked down, and said, "In the summer. And we know what he'll say, don't we? Military life is all he ever seemed to want." She stood up to leave, and so did Jim. "Well, good day. We'll let you know soon."

JoAnn and her mother, June, were standing in line outside the office and approached Jim and Susan. Her father remained seated, his head buried in a newspaper.

Jim noticed a bruise near June's right eye. She looked worn out. Even JoAnn seemed uneasy.

Susan greeted them with a conciliatory smile. "I'm terribly sorry, and I assure you it won't happen again. I've told Jim I don't want to see him anywhere near that plane again." She turned to him to reaffirm her will, then focused back on June's eye; Jim couldn't take his own off it. "Is everything okay?"

June, a little shy at first, cracked a smile. "Yes. Fine." She turned to Jim. "Anyway, I can tell he just loves it up there—like his father. Isn't that all that matters? I think he'll make a fine pilot someday."

Susan looked as if she'd swallowed a worm.

JoAnn gave him a furrowed brow, though she seemed to be chuckling inside.

Susan glanced over at JoAnn's father to say hello, but he remained indifferent, buried in his paper. June suddenly stiffened, as if someone had pumped her full of air. Her eyes became anxious.

Susan sighed at her. "You know, if you need help, you will call me now."

June nodded softly with a shallow smile, but Susan pressed her again. "It's okay. I had a fall in the yard, that's all."

It was unconvincing, even to Jim.

JoAnn kept her eyes on the ground.

Susan looked at her father again, swallowed her words, then turned to Jim. "Well, I have to go now. I'll see you at home."

"I'll be at the farm first, Mama. I have to start up some machinery for the auction," Jim said.

"Okay, don't be late." She said goodbye, then turned and started walking. "And stay away from that plane now, d'you hear?"

The principal interrupted from his office. "Mr. and Mrs. Johnson? Please come in."

JoAnn gave Jim one last look before disappearing into the room with her parents.

On his way out, he passed Susie, a cute brunette, though he also thought she was a little scrawny, as if she'd been stretched out at home. He kept walking when she sidled up and brushed his arm.

"You still owe me that ride in the plane, Jim boy."

"Yeah, sure. I'll, uh, be back in the air soon. How about, uh, next week?" That was all he could conjure up, though it would be impossible without gas or money.

She smiled broadly and marveled at him, which he liked. "I still can't believe you have your own plane. The rest of us walk everywhere."

Jim shrugged. It wasn't his plane, but why break the spell? "It's nice up there. Feels like you're on top of the world." He put on a smile. "And you're next in line."

She grabbed his arm. "Yeah? Wow! You know, we could fly to the Enchanted Rock. The stars are amazing at night."

JoAnn had mentioned a similar trip to Jim, but he couldn't remember where. That might be his ace in the hole, but he was sure the crop duster wouldn't be available for pleasure trips, even if it could go that far. He fantasized about taking the girls on a picnic together.

"Uh, sure. Sounds fun," he replied. "I'll think of something."

Susie pulled away with a friend while he walked on with a broad grin, eventually stopping at the school gates.

The entrance commanded a magnificent view of the surrounding terrain for several miles in almost every direction. Built recently, just like his neighborhood, it sat on a low hill and enjoyed an elevated vantage point. In a couple of months, bright purple lavender would carpet virtually the entire plain in one direction, and huge bales of hay would pepper the other.

He scanned the sky expectantly, but there were no planes today.

Reaching into a pocket, he pulled out a folded piece of paper that he had intended to show in the office but hadn't found the courage or the moment to do so. He unfolded it and looked at it, wondering what he should do. *Join the Navy*, it read, with a picture of three fighters flying in formation over the tall gray stern of a warship. He wasn't ready to give up on the idea, even though he knew his mama hadn't bought it—but his father would surely back him, wouldn't he?

CHAPTER 3 - FARMER BOY

Same afternoon

Dressed in a blue jumpsuit, Jim leaned into the engine block of a huge, pale-red Massey-Harris harvester. The machine, which looked like a giant mechanical insect with pipes and struts everywhere, had emerged from a six-month hibernation in the shed, and needed to be fired up. Drawn to mechanics, he saw it as a perfect way to learn and earn some money, while Lebbe was eager to help, fulfilling a promise to provide pastoral care in his father's absence. Jim was relieved he could talk to the man.

The farmer had stubbornly resisted the new machine revolution to save on labor, but that, along with all the surplus crops floating around the system, had nearly put him out of business. Now he had to sell some of his old equipment to pay off his debts. Even they were in high demand and already worth a small fortune. He needed the money.

Jim tightened a few bolts with a wrench. "Looks like there's some moisture in the carb here." He stood up and wiped his hands on a red rag from his back pocket. "I cleaned it out now, so it should work." He glanced at the farmhand in the cab. "Why don't you give it a shot? Fire it up."

Wilson, a middle-aged African-American in equally faded

gray overalls, started the Massey from the small cab on top. Jim leaned in again but backed away quickly as the engine sputtered with a coughing fit. Wilson shut it off and climbed down.

"They're shipping this fella out at first light. It's our last night with him once he's in bed," Jim said.

Wilson grabbed a broom and leaned on it. "I'll sure miss these machines. Wonderful, they are, and it's a damn shame they're going. I first drove that tractor out there when I was a boy on this farm."

Jim gave him an almost imperceptible nod to acknowledge the passing of an era. "We're going to need some room here to swing in the big loader. Then I think we're all set for the night once your tractor's inside too. You can lock up and take the keys back please."

He put his tools on the bench and asked, "So what's next, Wilson? Looks like there's a shrinking opportunity for sturdy hands like yours. New machines are coming in to replace folks like us. Someday they'll be running around out there on their own. But one thing's for sure," he said with a grin. "They're all gonna need fixing."

"You're good at that kind of thing, Jim. Is that what you're gonna do now? I thought you were off to college."

"I want to fly around the world, Wilson, but it looks like my mama ain't having it." As soon as he said those words, he wondered if she'd in fact been right about farming. Maybe he *was* born to work with his hands on the ground. He actually enjoyed overhauling machines, though maybe not as much as flying them. "Who knows? Maybe I can start a repair shop. I think I'm gonna need options, just in case." It sparked an idea. "Tell you what, we could do it together, you and I. You know how they work."

Wilson laughed it off like an old joke, and said, "Jim, you're too kind, but the new machines are beyond me. No, I can't see it. Anyway, I was planning to head south after the summer." He clarified his thoughts. "I'm not sure if I'll be back up here again."

Jim looked slightly surprised. "Are you sure? The segregationists still rule down there."

"Nothing's for sure, Jim. But my mama's not too good. I have to take care of the family. I don't know how we're going to pay it back, but I got to do something. Anyway, the last time I was sure about anything was when I was a little boy. And that's only 'cause I had a lot less to be sure about," he said, laughing again.

"Well, look me up if you're back and I'm still here."

Wilson acknowledged.

Jim turned to look outside. "Okay, is the other girl ready now? I think we'll put her right over there with her daddy. That'll give them room enough to swing around the trailer tomorrow. Shall we get to it?"

Wilson walked to the door, but stopped to lean on his broomstick again. He scanned the sky. Though it was still day, the moon was ghostly white in the light blue sky. "I've always wondered what it's like to fly like a bird. You like it up there, Jim?"

It was an unexpected question, and Jim wondered if he'd heard about the crop duster episode. "Best place in the world. You?"

"I'd have to break free of the world down here first. It'll be a long time before folks like me can do anything like that." His jovial self reappeared. "The mechanics might just think there's an oil leak somewhere, looking at me in the back seat." He roared at his own joke.

22

The self-deprecation impressed Jim. But, right or wrong, he couldn't have agreed more about how others might see Wilson's skin color. He walked to the door and stood beside his buddy, just as he caught sight of JoAnn's figure walking up the street toward them in the distance. Her lightness and poise captivated him immediately.

"My mama would probably kill me first before one of those planes could do any harm anyway," he said to Wilson, his eyes still on JoAnn. He muttered, almost to himself, "Besides, I have something I have to do now."

Wilson laughed again and said, "I can see that. I'll just look outside and bring the other young lady to the door." He handed over the broom and walked away toward the machines.

Jim followed him out slowly, wiped his hands on a rag, and stood, looking contentedly at the row of carefully parked equipment in the yard that he'd looked over the previous few evenings. He smoothed the ruffles in his jumpsuit, straightened his collar, and brushed his hair back with his grubby fingers until they felt clean.

He called for JoAnn, watching her every step as she approached the doors. She was wearing a knee-length light pink and white checked dress, tied in the middle with a thin black belt, and collared at the top.

They greeted each other shyly. She looked him over and pulled away with a chuckle.

"Greasy blue, huh?" she said.

Jim looked down at himself and apologized.

"And now, red lipstick too?" she said, looking up coyly at the mark she'd made on his left cheek.

Her arms were crossed over her books, which were held to her chest as if to protect them from the surrounding dirt.

23

"Come inside. I promise not to touch you," Jim said.

She agreed, then asked, though slightly bemused and not at all sounding like she's been offended, "So, just what did you think you were doing?"

"Yesterday? A fly-past," he said with a bright smile.

"A what?"

"I thought you might like to see the plane ... on your birthday."

"I expected to be in it, not looking up at it." She turned to look around the hangar. "So when are you taking me up?"

"You asked your father?"

"You know, it's a good thing he wasn't home yesterday. He would have seriously killed us both." She pulled away, still curious about her surroundings. "I guess you're grounded now?"

"Maybe ... well, okay. But I'm telling you, one day I'm gonna fly around the world in a fast jet. They're coming, you know."

She looked back at him, surprised. "Oh, really? And what did your mama and the principal say about that?"

Jim shook his head, agonizing for a moment over his indecision about the whole affair. He had not yet spoken to his father. "And you?"

"I just need to get away. Anywhere will do right now. It's a madhouse. But it'll be hard. Daddy says, over his dead body. He thinks I should be at home, taking care of the house, since Mama's not so well. She takes the brunt of everything." She shrugged. "I don't know if I can leave her alone."

JoAnn's candor surprised Jim. "So where would you go?"

"I don't know. Somewhere where I can help the world. There's so much to do. There's injustice everywhere." She paused.

"Help who?"

24

"I'll go to college and become a journalist. Maybe a photographer. People don't notice things unless you put them in their living rooms or under their noses."

"You want to write about things?"

"Yeah, people's rights, maybe."

Jim waited for clarification—he'd never heard of such a thing.

"You know? Rights for women and … well, people like him." She looked out the barn door.

"Who, Wilson?"

"Yeah."

"Wilson's doing just fine here, though the rise of the machines might have something to say about that. He works hard, and this ain't the Deep South. Though, he's thinking about going back home to his folks." Jim shrugged. The rights of others weren't his fight right now when he still had to settle his own future.

Seeing his cogs turn, JoAnn asked, "So, what are you going to do?"

"I'm working on it. But agri's always here if it falls through." Not wanting to bomb the moment or spill the beans on his idea to disappear into the Navy, Jim bit his tongue. "Right now I need to get this old stuff going."

"Why?"

"They're going under the hammer. The auction here's this weekend, and I promised I'd help get this old stuff started again."

"Oh, I thought you could walk me back." She smoothed her hair, as if that would make a difference.

"Can you wait a while?" He pointed to the machines. "That one out there's done, but I need to get this one going." He looked up at the large harvester. "All this equipment's going."

25

"Well, okay, but I can't stay long," JoAnn said.

She glanced around the dimly lit workshop as Jim walked over and jumped onto the bottom rung of the harvester's steps. With a leap that bypassed several levels, he swung into the cab with one hand and grabbed the railing. He groaned, twisting his wrist awkwardly. He winced and soothed it, sat down, flipped switches in the cab, then leaned forward to pull out a wiring loom from under the steering wheel.

JoAnn walked to a far corner of the shed, taking care not to touch anything. "What's this?"

Jim covertly nursed his wrist. "That's a side delivery rake." He looked up and saw her eyes shift to the next one. "And that's a swath turner." He fiddled with the starter while JoAnn scanned hay bales in another corner. His jacket was on top.

She stole a glance at him. "Are you going to the ball on Saturday?"

"I promised to come here and stay out all day. And I want to see what all this stuff is worth. I'll meet some people. Maybe get a break."

"A break?" JoAnn sounded surprised again.

"There's money to be made in these machines."

"You were off flying around the world a minute ago."

"Yeah. But, you know, this could still be an option." Jim had his hands in a loom under the dash, and added. "If Mama gets her way."

"Have you told her?"

"Nope. And I'm not going to encourage her, even though I'm sure she'll be very happy for it. Said so, loud and clear, in that office."

Jim glanced at a tractor parked in line outside, his hands still fiddling under the steering wheel.

26

JoAnn suddenly stepped away as the machine sputtered and smoked her with exhaust. He stopped the engine, grinned, and swung back down from the cab, still rubbing his wrist. "Listen, why don't you come by the auction this weekend? It'll be interesting."

"Sorry, can't. Daddy's taking the family to lunch with a business partner. He needs the deal. And Ricky's over too."

"It's only the morning. You'll be home for lunch, I promise." He froze, picturing Bruno for a moment, then asked, "Ricky? Who's Ricky?"

"Oh, no one." She let him hang for a moment, then said, "My nephew from Michigan. He's about this high." She floated a hand just above her right knee. "Anyway, will you take me home now?"

Jim grinned broadly again as an idea popped into his head. "Sure. But I need a favor first. A quick one before we go?" He looked at the bales in the corner and grabbed her wrist.

She looked at them too, chuckled, and pulled back. "No, Jim Cobb. What are you saying? You're not getting me to do anything like that."

"Go on. It'll be fun. It's easy. I'll show you how." He looked up at the cab and came clean. "Just turn the key up there. The seat's comfortable, I promise. And it's spotless ... well, for farm hands anyway."

She rolled her eyes and relented with a grin of her own.

"Don't worry. It's just like the little cockpit in the airplane. Pretend you're in the air, just like you wanted."

"Oh, is that how you make up?" She looked around the barn, took a deep breath, and offered him her books. Holding them away from his greasy overalls, he took them to the back, brushed the counter to spread the dirt, and set them down gently.

27

JoAnn was still figuring out how to climb aboard the machine when he came up behind her to help. He gave her a smile, which she returned, and gently lifted her up to the first rung. He returned to the engine.

"It's the big one. Turn the big key, then press the red button," he said, looking down into the cylinder block on one knee.

The harvester sputtered to life as JoAnn cranked the motor, half-filling the hangar with brown-black smoke.

He yelled over the noise with a wave of his hand, "Okay, that's it. Turn it off."

She twisted the key, stood up, and scanned for the fastest way down while Jim checked cable connections and squeezed a coupling tighter. He opened the doors wider to let in some fresh air.

JoAnn squealed behind him. He swung around to see that she'd lost her footing and rushed over, grabbing her by the waist and gently turning her around until she was back on the first rung. She stopped breathing for a moment as they stood face-to-face. "I was going to say, come down backwards." He couldn't help but grin.

JoAnn was in his arms, looking down into his eyes. Her face softened. She brushed a finger across his lips and kissed him gently, beaming shyly as he lifted her off the step and set her down gently. She straightened her frills.

"I'm sorry I kept you," Jim said.

JoAnn nodded with a glow and went to fetch her books from the back. Jim's eyes followed her as she headed for the door. He took off his overalls, grabbed his jacket, and handed the barn keys to Wilson over a fence on their way home.

He felt a perfect little bubble forming around them as they walked home, even as he agonized over whether or not to reveal his idea about joining the Navy.

CHAPTER 4 - GONE

Same evening

Jim had already lost his smile when he saw an unfamiliar black sedan parked in front of his house.

Just twenty minutes earlier, JoAnn's father had been engaged in a heated argument, so loud that it could be heard on the street as Jim and JoAnn arrived at her home. To Jim, the place looked tired up close, with faded windows and peeling paint.

"Where is she?" the man yelled. He'd been at the bottle, and her mother was in trouble.

JoAnn hurried across the yard and Jim followed. June was distraught as she opened the door and quietly ushered JoAnn inside, signaling for her to go up to her room immediately.

JoAnn gave him one last desperate look over her shoulder before she disappeared up the stairs after another round of screaming from her father.

Jim tried to peer over June's shoulder. JoAnn's sister, Eve, was hurrying around holding a small child close to her chest. "Is everything okay, Mrs. Johnson?"

June nodded from behind the half-closed door then shut it without saying a word.

He stood stunned for a moment, then continued on his way

home, only to be doubly startled when he saw a uniformed Air Force officer and chaplain at his own front door. He hurried up the path, knowing that their appearance meant only one thing, though he wished desperately that he was wrong.

Susan held the door open, her face blank with shock. He asked what was going on. The chaplain had a sympathetic face, though it looked strained. The officer's eyes were streaming and he struggled to speak. He could have broken down the moment he said, "Shall we go in?"

Jim's heart was pounding as they walked into the living room. He stood next to his mama, who sat quietly on the edge of an armchair. She looked down at the floor, knowing what was coming. Jim steeled himself.

The officer, still barely able to speak, recited, "The chief of staff has entrusted me to express his deep regret that Lieutenant Commander Cobb went missing in action, and is presumed dead while on a mission over Communist airspace six weeks ago to this day. The chief of staff extends his deepest sympathies to you and your family, Mrs. Cobb."

A long silence followed.

Susan's eyes were wet and still glued to the floor. "Six weeks? Where did he go? What was he doing?"

The officer swallowed. "Ma'am, Lieutenant Commander Cobb went missing on reconnaissance. The Soviets have not accounted for him."

"How do you know that? That he's dead?" Jim asked.

"The wreckage of his plane was sighted, sir, and it was determined there was no chance of a survivor."

"But the Communists must have him. Have you asked them?" demanded Susan.

"Our government has been pressing the Soviets, ma'am."

31

"He must be somewhere in Russia. You must look for him," Jim insisted.

The officer apologized.

Jim and his mama stared at them both, but no one in the room dared speak. Susan's eyes welled up. She walked to the window and looked out, as if Jim's father might just walk up and put an end to some terrible confusion. Her left hand reached for the window sill, and her right hand covered her face.

"Sir, ma'am, is there anyone who can stay with you in this time of need?" the chaplain asked.

Jim said there wasn't, though it was barely audible under his breath.

"Is there a clergyman in the family or a minister who can help you? Or another family member nearby?"

Jim shook his head and went to hold his mama. They hugged, then she ran upstairs.

Barely five minutes had passed before he showed the men back to the door. They said the Air Force would be in touch to arrange a funeral or memorial service, depending on whether or not they found his father.

He was numb at the door as the car pulled away. They had come like a swift punch to the nose, but the pain hadn't yet hit.

Across the street, Wilman looked strangely Red, as still as a scarecrow in his window again. Why was he spying on the comings and goings from behind his veiled curtains? It seemed very un-American. He had to be hiding something. And what did he do in the teachers' union office anyway? Was he one of those Communist sympathizers that Senator McCarthy of Wisconsin was trying to weed out of public service? Jim was sure the news of his father would spread through town quickly, and resolved to watch the man like a hawk. He'd call the police the minute he saw any suspicious behavior.

He closed the door, angry that the Reds were being allowed to infect the world. If he and others didn't step up to stop them now, who would? He rushed back to his room and pulled out a folded newspaper clipping explaining the Navy's Holloway Plan. That was how he'd fight the scourge and maybe, somehow, find out what had really happened to his father, even if it was the Air Force that lost him.

CHAPTER 5 - ENLIST

The Next Morning

Dogs baying, their sharp teeth bared. Leashed by men—soldiers. Hunting me. Why no faces? Snarling dogs. About to pounce. Move! Go! Go!

Jim heard his own groan, surprisingly loud, with the nightmare still fresh in his mind as he awoke. He looked around the dark room, expecting to see his mama. But nothing moved except for the pumping of his adrenaline-filled veins.

The clock said four a.m. He laid his head back down on the pillow and thought about his father, the reel of terror still rolling from his sleep.

Then the door flew open and Susan burst in.

She was at the stove later that morning and didn't immediately look at Jim when he walked into the kitchen. He sat down at the small square breakfast table, poured some water, picked up cutlery, and pulled over a plate of waffles. He drizzled on a drop of maple syrup.

Susan glanced over her shoulder and said they were out of milk and that she would get some in town later in the morning.

Jim's head stayed down, but he'd seen her troubled eyes.

She walked over and put a hand on his. "Do you want to see someone?" Her voice was hoarse and she cleared her throat.

Jim shook his head.

Susan looked exhausted and said she was going up the street to mail some letters to let the family know what had happened. She'd been up all night. "Will you come with me, Jim?"

He closed his eyes with his head still down. "I can't."

"It's okay. School knows you're not coming."

He took a deep breath. "I've decided, Mama."

Susan looked surprised. "Decided? Decided what?"

"I'm not going to Tarleton."

She was quietly confused.

"I have to go and find out what happened to Daddy."

"Go? Find out? Where?"

Jim was silent for several seconds. "I'm going to the Navy recruiting station."

Susan froze, then sat down. "Jim, you don't have to decide that right now."

"You said it yourself, Mama. We have to fight for freedom. That's what he did. Now I have to do my part."

She gripped his hand. "What if they send you out there, Jim, wherever he was?"

He bit into a waffle on his plate and ate it quickly.

"Jim, we talked about this. Why don't you wait? There might be some news."

He didn't answer.

Susan sighed. "Stop it, Jim. You're scaring me. What if I lose you too?"

He stood up, looked down at his half-eaten breakfast, and cleared his mouth. He finally looked up at her. "I have to do it, Mama. Or the Communists will take over everything."

He waited for an answer, but Susan was at a loss. He turned to leave.

"Jim, sit down and eat your breakfast, will you?" She stood up quickly and went back to the stove. "I'll make some eggs. Just give it some time. College can wait. They all can."

"It'll be open soon." Jim turned and pushed the chair under the table. "Sorry, Mama, but I have to go." He turned to leave again.

Susan was stunned. "You haven't eaten anything, Jim. Just sit down now, will you?"

But he was already gone.

CHAPTER 6 - ALBUMIN

Same morning

The morning's heat and a fifteen-mile bus ride had already worn Jim down by the time he arrived at the recruiting office. The brightly colored terraced building looked rather unambitious. Built of brick, they had squeezed it in between the General Post Office and a cobbler's shop. Hung above the dark doorway was a three-quarter arch with the words *Enlist Here*.

A trio of young men were waiting outside and looked undecided about whether or not to enter. Next to them, propped up against the wall, was a large billboard proclaiming that *The Red Menace Could Be Anywhere* and that people should *Report All Suspected Communist Activity*. It couldn't have been the Navy's, Jim thought, but they hadn't taken it down either.

He paused across the street, weighing his own decision to enlist and feeling like he should just march in there and demand they get his father back. As for suspects, he could just rat out old Wilman, figuring that the man might be gone by nightfall.

As the trio went inside, he swallowed hard, crossed the street, and looked inside the window first.

Jim remained apprehensive as he entered the small, shop-sized, high-ceilinged room. In the far right corner was a wooden desk with a typewriter, paper trays, and a telephone. A fan on the table barely managed to swing its small arc. Behind it sat a huge, uniformed naval officer who looked like he could fill the room if he stood up. He faced forward, processing paperwork.

The officer gave him a quick glance and told him to take a seat, which he did, to the left, and behind four others who were already waiting; they glanced at him to signal their position in line. Next to him was a slim, pale teenager who hardly looked like Navy material to Jim.

He sat down and looked around the room. They'd painted the walls a light military gray. A door led to another office at the back, with two more rooms down the hall.

"Do you think everyone in the Navy has to be an ace swimmer?" the guy next to him whispered, looking like a bundle of frayed nerves before a test.

Jim hadn't thought of that—he'd only imagined Navy life to be above the water and suddenly wondered if he was in the right place. He looked around for a clue. What did a sailor or submariner look like, anyway? "I came for the planes. You?"

The guy leaned forward, looking pleased. "Me too. I'm Frank."

Jim felt relieved. "Well, I guess the nearest water for us will be up in the clouds."

Frank leaned further forward and whispered, "Never been on an airplane. You?"

"Recon it's the best job in the world."

"I drove a tractor when I was thirteen. Is flying a plane different?"

Frank, with his slight build, looked like he might get lost in a small cockpit. Jim winked and said with a grin, "I think you'll fit right in up there."

Frank's face lit up as the officer called him. He hurried to the desk and sat down on the near side, looking awestruck.

"Okay, so today you'll do the paper tests," the officer said, in a booming voice. "We'll need a sample today. And you'll be back for the physicals tomorrow. Any questions?"

Frank looked thrilled. He nodded and agreed immediately when handed a little cup.

"Okay, this way, please." The officer stood and, almost ducking in the doorway, led Frank to the back. Jim's bench stood up together, leaned forward, and peered quietly down the hall behind them. The next room contained neatly arranged desks on which other recruits were scribbling test papers. The line quickly dropped to their seats as the giant strode back again.

Twenty minutes later, Jim began his own application once the line had cleared.

"Why do you want to join the Navy, son?" the officer asked, still looking at his papers.

Sitting across from him, Jim searched his mind for the right words. Remembering the sign outside, he said, "To, uh, beat the Communists, sir."

"Good answer. Good." The giant continued to shuffle and mark his papers without a reaction. Jim was about to tell the story of his father when the man repeated the application process that Jim had already heard several times in line.

They gave him a paper test in the next room after he filled a little pee cup. He scanned the questions, which were all multiple choice, except for a handful that needed wordy answers. The exam began with English and moved on to technical, which looked a lot like physics. That test might have stumped others, but Jim was fine, for he hoped to be studying engineering at Navy College anyway.

Despite a shaky start in which he couldn't figure out if *a rose is a rose is a rose* needed punctuation, he was confident he would pass the paper tests and felt resolved about enlisting on his way back home.

First stop was JoAnn's. He needed to tell her the news about his father. He hadn't had the heart to lean on her the night before. She had her own problems, but maybe things had calmed down in her house by now.

When she came to the door, he explained what had happened and why he wasn't at school. She said she had called at his house and already knew. He revealed that he'd been at the Navy recruiting station. She said that his mama had told her everything.

She still looked shocked. "You're not going to college?"

"I will, but with the Navy. I'm going to see if I can find out what happened to my father. Somehow, I have to try."

"Why don't you take some time? Now's not the time to decide on something like that," she said; and anyway, he still had to finish school.

He explained that he'd be gone for seven years, though it dawned on him immediately that that meant basically forever. He saw moisture in her eyes, tried to backtrack, and added that tomorrow they would, "feel inside his pants," and that he would, "find out if he had the balls for the job anyway."

They parted with a frigid, awkward goodbye.

* * *

The next day, Jim was early and braced for the physical.

He had no particular ailments, allergies, or intolerances to speak of, and his eyesight was perfect, as far as he knew. There had been no problems with his hearing, although his school counselor said listening could use some work.

He was lined up with several other shirtless men in the farthest room, measured five feet nine with a forty-two inch chest, and weighed one hundred and fifty pounds, which was well over the minimum.

The dreaded curtains opened. He looked at the medics anxiously as he waited, then steeled himself as a man emerged sheepishly from behind the curtain and ran past a row of curious eyes in the line.

Another medic came out to get some papers and ushered Jim into the booth. He sat on a stool and gave his temperature, blood pressure, and pulse.

The medic smiled sardonically. "We do that first. The physical throws them off."

Jim's breath shallowed at the order to strip down to his shorts. He undressed, keeping his eyes on the wall in front of him.

"Now, drop your shorts," the medic said.

Jim's temperature rose, but he complied, clutching his breath tightly.

The man continued, "Okay, now turn around and touch your toes."

Jim's heart skipped a beat. He spun around quietly and squatted tensely with his arms hanging down like a great ape. A small eternity passed as the medic quietly observed Jim from behind. He dared not look to either side.

"Now spread your legs," the man said.

Jim's face reddened as he remained prone for a few moments. What on earth was the man looking for? Communists?

The medic scribbled on a clipboard, then called a colleague from outside the curtain. Great, Jim thought. Why not charge a dollar apiece for the show?

"They look okay to you?" the medic asked.

The second man agreed and disappeared again.

Still writing, the medic finally said, "Okay. The fun's over. Get your clothes on." Suddenly, it all seemed very routine.

Relief washed over Jim. He jumped to it, then sat in the chair, regained his dignity, and wondered if there was a problem. Humbled, he asked, "Anything interesting up there?"

Without answering, the medic reached over and levered Jim's head in every direction. He instructed Jim to cough, open his mouth wide, and say "Ahhh." The medic pounded on his knees, then on his chest and his back, while listening for his heartbeat and breath. Curiously, he asked, "Have you ever had tetanus?"

"Uh, no," Jim said, not quite sure what that was. "I don't think they test for that where I live."

The medic thought for a moment, then signed the physical sheet. "That means you've never had tetanus. You're free to go."

Mightily reassured, Jim bolted for the bathroom, not daring to look back at the line.

He stepped up to the urinal with a huge sigh. "Goddamn, that's a relief," he said with a cackle. "I don't know what he found back there. I was worried they were about to dive right in." He glanced to his right and saw a worried-looking Frank.

"Albumin," Frank said flatly.

"Albumin?" repeated Jim, his face pained as he tried to remember where he'd heard such a word.

"Albumin. In my pee." Frank shrugged and looked down at the beaker he was holding to his pecker. "Two samples, both with albumin. Said I was dehydrating. Kidneys could be a problem."

Jim thought, then said, "Well, just drink lots of water. Wait a few hours and try again." It seemed like a reasonable suggestion. He went back to his business and the stream flowed.

Frank sighed and said, "I did that yesterday. And I drank all night." He looked down. "No albumin today, but the specific gravity's too low. It's my last chance."

Jim screeched to a halt mid-flow. "Look, I, uh, have an unfinished load here." He forced a contorted smile. "Would you like? Do you want me to, you know? Fill her up?" It seemed like an uncompelling gift, but it was all he could offer. He winced, half expecting it to be thrown back in his face and looked down at Frank's collector.

"You okay?" Frank asked.

Jim strained. "Well, I can't hold on much longer here ... Oh! Yes. Yes! No! There's no albumin here. Not in the Cobb family. I just checked out, and I think they really liked it." Still holding tight, he puffed out a few quick, shallow breaths, and put out a hand to press Frank for an answer.

Frank finally handed him the cup.

"No problem. Just give me a minute here." Jim snapped it into place and relaxed with a big exhale. A steadying hand went on the wall.

After a moment, Jim returned the lukewarm, half-filled cup. "Here you go. You show them. They might even think we're brothers, you and I." He zipped up again with a grin. "Oh, and I won't be needing that back."

But Frank still looked dejected.

"What? Not enough? Well, I, uh, there was only a drop left. I'd already started; you saw that." He looked down at the urinal and fumbled to reopen his zipper. "I could squeeze a little harder. I had a fair amount of—"

"I'm two pounds underweight," Frank said.

Jim stopped.

"Not quite the hundred and fifteen they want. The water helped, but it all came out before the weigh-in," Frank added.

Jim thought as he zipped up again. "Two pounds, huh?" He mulled a bit more, straightened his clothes, then said with a big smile, "Okay, come with me. You feeling peckish?"

The pair handed in Frank's last chance sample and disappeared from the recruiting office. For the next hour, Frank scarfed down two pounds of cantaloupe and washed it down with two large vanilla milkshakes with Jim's help. They returned just in time for Frank's one o'clock weigh-in.

Bingo. The plan worked.

The recruiting officer called them back to the front desk at around two.

The friendly giant spoke again. "Jim Cobb? Frank Baum? Today is your lucky day. Congratulations. You can now join the haul-away plan. Raise your right hand like this and sign here on the line. Both of you."

Courtesy of Admiral James Holloway, the officer swore in Jim, who was not yet eighteen and a half, and Frank, who was just a month older, to the United States Naval Reserve.

Now, Jim just had to extract himself from school with a quarter still to go.

CHAPTER 7 - MARINO

A week later, April 1950

A week later, Jim and Frank received their papers to enter Holloway's Naval Aviation College Program at the University of Southern California. The March intake had already begun, and they still had space. Susan, and Jim's school resisted, though they quickly realized that it was futile to stop the headstrong Jim from pursuing his ambitions. He argued that college was college, and he had no entrance exams to hold him back either way. Naval College had accepted his GPA, so surely that was that.

Susan waved him off with a small bundle of food and clean clothes, though he was sure they would feed and clothe him for the next few years and he wouldn't be needing them.

He said goodbye to JoAnn one day when her father wasn't home. She was doing laundry. He was obviously excited about his new venture, although he felt a little selfish, adding that he'd be right back if he flunked out anyway. He suggested that she could visit him at college. She said she didn't think that was possible with school and whatever came next. It felt like a final goodbye. Now, he feared, that bozo Bruno would have a free run at JoAnn unless he could keep her attention from afar.

He and his new buddy, Frank, took the long train to California that spring, expecting they would return to Texas some day to finish their training.

The college had them sign contracts in the first week, promising to commission them as midshipmen if they succeeded. The Navy provided uniforms, a taste of Navy life in the Officer Candidate Training Unit, and housed them with a group of roommates on West 36th Street.

Eight bunks stood in two rows with a wide walkway between their feet. Pale green walls continued up to the roof, supported by columns about ten feet apart. Everything matched the color of their clothes, and all the bunks were like identical slabs of brown chocolate with white pillows against the walls. The floor was bare and spotless. Just making his bed to Navy standards seemed to provide Jim with a positive start each day.

One morning in his second week, he was still getting used to a close-cropped haircut. The Navy had quickly banished every frill from his life, and his head felt a pound lighter with all the dark locks gone. His new khaki uniform looked impressively tailored in the mirror, and a whole new quality for him. But not everyone was so lucky—everything seemed to hang loose on Frank. He wasn't getting any thinner, but he just couldn't eat enough to fill it out.

A cadet yelled from across the room as they awaited inspections. "Five minutes, boys." Jim looked at himself in the mirror again while he watched another group of cadets out the window. They were falling out of the next building in all whites.

"Fifty dollars! Can you imagine that?" gushed Frank, waving a pair of boots he was shining at the end of his bunk across the way. It looked like the first pair he'd ever polished.

"Don't spend it all at once. Although I don't see how you can avoid that," Jim said.

"Uh, that's fifty a month, not a week, Frank," another cadet said, tightening his belt at the next bunk.

"Yeah. I know that. But I never had five bucks at the end of the week serving behind the old man's counter. And a beer's only a half-buck down here."

"Don't let them catch you slugging those back. You'll get punched out."

"Punched out? Sounds a little violent."

"You know, punched out?"

Frank didn't get it. He kept polishing his boots.

The cadet rolled his eyes. "An ejector seat?"

"Oh, yeah. Don't try that, buddy. You'll be even shorter," said another.

The cadet put on a shirt that looked identical to all the others. "Who you calling shorty, shorty?"

"You calling me a midge?" Frank looked up at Jim. "Hey, he called me a midge. Did you hear that?"

"Well, look at you," the cadet said. "The lieutenant's gonna have to look under the bunk when he comes in."

Frank was still in shorts and a T-shirt at the end of his bed. "Who, Marino?" He half-laughed as he polished away. "You know he has a degree in yelling from Marine School. Did you know that? They must have shouting matches at the end of the year. We just had a regular sports day."

Seven cadets suddenly sprung up in unison and stood as straight as posts at the foot of their bunks. Undone buttons were quickly looped. They straightened their heads and shoulders like statues.

Lieutenant Marino, also in khakis, was standing in the door-way. A tight black strap under his chin held a dark brown hat that

47

hid his domed head. He walked slowly toward them, tapping his heels, and stopped motionless at the head bunk.

The silence was thick enough to cut with a knife, until Frank, still pulling on his boots, hobbled onto one foot and stood awkwardly at the end of his own bunk.

The room fell silent again as the lieutenant moved down the center aisle, his boots tap-tapping with every step. He stopped in front of Frank's face and studied it—his own, distorted, as if he'd swallowed some terrible medicine. "You ain't heard nothing yet, puke!" he roared, the words ripping through every ear in the room like a foghorn.

Marino's hawk eyes scanned the line for another transgression. Then he began to yell. "Now listen up. I'm going to mold you ragtag newcomer fly-boys into something that even the Marines might recognize as officers. But don't bet your measly fifty dollars on it." The tirade faded into an equally deafening silence again. With a few slow steps, he stopped in front of Jim and stared him quietly in the face. "I guarantee that some of you will not make it out of here in an officer's uniform. I will not spend the American people's money just to keep you busy if you have no business being here." He turned back to Frank and maxed the volume again. "Do you understand?"

The cadets returned a rather feeble, "Yes, sir."

"I said, do you understand?" boomed the lieutenant.

"Yes, sir!"

On the move again, he continued. "I promise to weed you out of here before the bank opens for business." He looked down at Frank's boots, stopped, and froze, as if he'd just seen a pair of whaling boats.

Jim, his head braced in place, glanced sideways with his eyes. Frank's boots still looked dull and grubby around the soles.

Polishing boots, they told him, was a painstaking, millimeter-by-millimeter affair. They would tolerate no less.

"Were you never taught to shine your shoes at home, boy?" Marino said.

Frank looked dazed.

"On the floor. I'll have twenty push-ups!"

Frank dropped like a rag doll and churned out reps as the lieutenant walked back up the line, inspecting more shoes. Frank slowed quickly and looked as though he would keel over like a sunken vessel when he couldn't have pushed out more than ten of his quota.

Marino looped around the top of the line and strolled back toward Jim. He stopped and looked him up and down. "You just follow in your buddy's footsteps there, and you'll be on the first train straight back to Texas. You hear me?"

Jim's face flushed while Frank continued to push like a piston about to seize.

Marino went back to the door.

"Frank Baum!" he shouted. "I don't know what I've done in my life to deserve you. I'll have another twenty! Then I want all of you ready, out in the field."

Twenty-five minutes later, the cadets were on the lawn overlooking the Coliseum, jumping stars in all whites like the previous batch Jim had seen outside his window. The blazing sun had drenched them in sweat. Marino paced the line like a drill instructor with his German shepherd. A chief petty officer stood guard.

As he jumped, Jim saw a long line in front of a dentist's trailer in the distance to the left. It was another batch of new cadets waiting their turn to have fillings, and wisdoms extracted—and

49

all in one sitting, just as Jim and his group had experienced two days earlier.

"Think Dr. No-Nuts is still looking for his crotch?" Frank said, panting hard as they jumped.

"I should have booted him too, drill or no drill," replied another cadet, puffing beside him.

Jim remembered standing third in line in front of the long, rectangular, prefabricated dentist's booth, agonizing over the wait for one tooth fairy when there should have been two. The lair stood on stilts, with two small windows just above head height on the long side. The steps to the entrance were in front and on the thin right edge of the building.

Apprehension muted the line, except for one cadet at the head. In a fret, Danny offered the first spot to any takers, claiming that they had recently okayed his gnashers, that he didn't need to be here, and that someone had made a mistake. But despite the long, tedious wait, no one rushed in to switch places with him.

Danny climbed the stairs in a mild sweat after the previous patient left in a hurry. Three minutes later, an energetic debate began inside the thin-walled prefab. They urged Danny to open his mouth wider, stop biting something, and put his head back down. After several bouts of anguished whining, someone inside howled and groaned in distress. Metal clanged and utensils scattered across the floor.

Three cadets in line outside jumped for a small window as rapid footsteps shuffled inside and the dental assistant ordered Danny to sit back down.

A moment later, the entrance door flew open and a man in a white coat hobbled out, whimpering in agony with his crotch in his hand. He limped down the steps and staggered across the lawn to the main building.

Jim and two cadets leaned toward the open door as Danny burst out, completely drenched in sweat. He stopped on the landing, holding his jaw and rubbing his wrist. He, too, ran to the main building after an anguished glance at the line. The assistant rushed to the door and called after him, then stormed back inside.

The cadets were beside themselves as they were relieved for the rest of the morning. Jim remembered gripping the armrests so tightly that a nail separated from the end of his thumb as he lay down for his slot with a replacement dentist that same afternoon.

"He must sound just like his wife," Frank said, now jumping stars on the field to Jim's left.

"He should have known where not to stand, don't you think? Can't be the first time," Jim replied.

"I think they should all just be castrated. For their own safety," Frank said in a female squeak.

The cadets snickered until one interrupted. "Hey, look, they're putting in the centrifuge. Did you see that? I read about it."

A large hoist lifted a long, crisscrossed arm into a huge new building in the distance near the dentist's cabin.

"I want to give that thing a spin," Frank said. "See how many G's I can pull. I bet I can do all nine. How many does a pilot need these days?"

"Nine? You'll be a puddle, buddy," Jim said.

The drill suddenly changed to squats, which silenced the chatter.

* * *

College began about four weeks later.

First, they got a repeat of high school physics, chemistry, and math. It all seemed like a new language to Frank, and he leaned heavily on Jim.

And just as it was getting started, they suddenly slammed on the brakes. On May nineteenth, the Navy announced the end of Holloway. Without warning, Jim and Frank's dreams seemed stillborn when the Navy revealed that they would be let go of by the end of June.

CHAPTER 8 - FLAMING GLORY

Late-May 1950, California

The following week, Jim and Frank decided to join the Naval Reserve Officer Training Corps at USC, a long-standing program that had been interrupted by Holloway's generous offer. The Navy agreed to honor their college commitment, and as compensation for an inconvenient holding pattern while they got started, Marino promised them a ships tour at Hunter's Point in San Francisco.

Once aboard a huge moored vessel, they found themselves rewarded with the opportunity to learn paint stripping in the crew quarters until classes resumed the following month. Frank revealed that he felt compelled to join the Navy as he chipped away at each fleck, explaining that he came from a military family, though he recognized that he didn't have the physical stature of a Marine. On the other hand, he was convinced that smaller pilots burned less gas, so he was actually perfectly built for the air.

"I should have just enough money to get home for a day," Jim said, though he knew the Navy did not allow leave until after college.

"I don't understand. How did you get leave already? We just

got here."

"Father's memorial, finally. Someone said I could just go."

"Sorry to hear that, Jim. There's been no news?"

Jim shook his head sadly. He hadn't yet felt the finality of his father's passing and his mama knew the memorial would not bring closure.

He'd written to JoAnn to ask if she would come. He asked about the end of school and said he still remembered the picnic trip they'd planned, and promised to fly her to the stars when he returned. To belittle Bruno, he reminded her that a fancy car just wouldn't do the trick.

On the day of the service, JoAnn gave him a badge that read, *Whatever you're doing, please keep doing.* She'd seen it, thought of him, and said he should fasten it next to his father's DC-3 pin. She said she also thought about the picnic at the same time as him, and marveled at how they thought alike. She couldn't wait to get to the University of Texas in Austin to start her journalism course. In a reply to his letter, she also explained that she wasn't that into Bruno, and that he had already wrapped his car around a tree anyway.

By June, Jim and his buddies were classified as non-rated seamen, and little seemed to have changed. Physics, math, and English classes continued in between seamanship, navigation, and ordnance. Most of the time they perfected salutes, chivalry, and impeccable dress that were becoming of an officer. He sometimes wondered if the Navy actually had any planes to fly or conflicts to fight, and whether he should have chosen the Air Force instead.

Then, one morning in late June, news that America had piled into the Korean War in support of the United Nations, startled him. He sat with his roommates listening to the radio. The reporter said that northern Communist forces had invaded somewhere called the thirty-eighth parallel, that the Soviets — and maybe even China — were behind it, and their goal was to paint the entire Far East Red.

* * *

Fall 1950

They continued to amuse, bemuse, and entertain Marino throughout the summer, and in the fall they learned that the few remaining Holloway cadets had been given indefinite assignments as they watched the Korean front line move up and down the country like a concertina. The enemy had almost pushed America and the United Nations back south into the sea from where they had come. The Communists looked unassailable. Then, in a stroke of genius, McArthur drove his troops all the way back up to the northern border with China, which piled in and forced a full-scale retreat back south again. Truman threatened to unleash America's A-bombs again, and some of Jim's roommates argued that this was a perfectly reasonable next step, just as it had been in Japan.

Frank shook his head in disbelief as he swept an office hallway with a wide broom that morning. Jim, preoccupied with a new letter he had written to JoAnn, advanced with a mop and bucket right behind him. They were paying their dues for not folding the head end on their bunks to the proper length, according to Marino.

He'd sent her a photo with Frank and their buddies that morning, reiterating that he missed her and that it felt like a lifetime since he'd last touched anything soft and warm.

55

Remorsefully, he apologized for leaving home so suddenly and wished they could pick up where they had left off. He asked about her college and life at home.

"My mother thought we were free of such troubles," Frank said to Jim, as they worked.

Jim was still on his own planet as he mopped the floor.

"The war," Frank said, bringing him back. "And the Navy's fighting, too, by the look of it—and here we are perfecting the crease in our pants."

"Oh, yeah." Jim sighed. The Navy did seem to be fixated on tailored clothes, table manners, and endless jumping-jacks. "You're right. It's time to put down the silverware and do what's necessary. We have to keep the Reds in line."

"You want to go out there and kick some ass?"

Jim was still sensitive about leaving JoAnn and home, let alone going to the other side of the world. He dipped his mop and swept it across the solid red tile floor. "It's somewhere near China, isn't it?"

"Yeah. It'll be chopsticks practice tomorrow."

Jim relaxed, laughed, and glanced up the long, empty hallway, dimly lit by a faint chandelier and the light of a drizzly day streaming in through double doors at the far end. Twenty yards were done. They'd just passed the office of the Professor of Naval Science on the right. The floor outside Marino's room on the left was still wet and shiny.

Jim pushed his mop into a small corner and stopped to look. "We're almost done."

Frank looked around a larger bend in the hall. "Marino didn't say over there, did he?"

"Best not to risk it."

Frank glanced at the left bend behind them. "It looks good

already. And he doesn't go that way. He won't even notice."

"Let's just do it. I don't feel like another round of chipping paint. Do you?" Jim said.

"We've got to be quick. I still have to finish Professor Pluto's work," said Frank, sweeping quickly, while Jim swung his mop with wide wall-to-wall arcs around the corner.

"Naval history?" Jim asked.

"Yep, and solid geometry," Frank replied. "Did I tell you I used to make those little warships? Guns too."

"Yeah?"

"We cut and painted balsa. Water got through some of them. A few became subs," Frank said.

"I made airplanes in grade school," Jim said.

Frank nodded with delight. "You got them to fly?"

"Ten yards with an engine and a little prop up front. Used Mama's rubber bands and pins to hold it together while the glue dried. Took hours to cut out the pieces."

Frank said his paper airplanes never flew straight.

Jim continued. "I had tissue paper for the skin. Banana oil to tighten it. But I had to be careful with the band. Too tight and it broke. I should have told Mama they were hers."

"Tell her now. Get it off your chest, buddy, or it'll be the last thing you remember on your dying day."

"I had too many planes hanging from my ceiling. One day I lit a few on fire and threw them out the window. Flaming Glory was the best."

"Like those kamikaze Japs?" Without waiting for an answer, Frank stopped and looked around again. They'd cleared another few yards. "I say we're done. Let's go."

At that moment, a blue ball bounced and echoed down the hall near the entrance. Marino's German shepherd came bounding in after it, giving chase with billows of doggy breath. The ball rebounded off a wall and rolled across the floor toward an office door. Dripping saliva, the dog bit, stopped to look at them with perked ears, then shook a mist of muddy water off its back.

Frank groaned with his hands on his head as Jim approached the wet dog.

Marino strode in through the door with muddy boots, stopped, and looked around the hall. "Here, buddy." The dog trotted back to him, drooling over the ball in her teeth.

Jim and Frank stopped to salute as Marino walked into his office.

He paused at the door and turned the handle. "I've never seen this hallway looking so filthy in all my years here." He looked up at Jim and Frank, then pointed to the entrance. "Start over there. I want it so clean you can eat your dinner off the floor."

Marino disappeared into his office and immediately threw the ball down the hall toward Jim and Frank. The dog pounced on it, knocking over Jim's dirty water bucket and splashing the floor at his feet. She caught the ball, sniffed them excitedly, and disappeared into Marino's office. The door slammed shut behind her.

CHAPTER 9 - O-COURSE

One Year later, October 1951, Pensacola, Florida

A year later, by the fall of fifty-one, Jim and Frank had mastered cleaning, cutlery, and dressing. They'd also passed the engineering curriculum, survived Lieutenant Marino, and had finally finished college.

They, and another two-score cadets (out of the sixty recruits who started), were shunted off to Naval Air Station Pensacola to find out if the Navy would finally give them a seat in an airplane. Pre-flight heralded much promise if they made it through the initial month of selectives.

At first, Jim felt like he was back in his old crop-duster, soaring high in the Navy's Stearman. Frank revealed the moment he saw a picture of a Boeing F4B-4 at the age of ten and first wanted to fly for the military. He explained how he rode his bicycle a few miles to a small airfield, sat on the tracks, and watched in awe at the flying activity. Jim said he liked the polished aluminum Ryan ST, an open-cockpit two-seater, and hoped he would fly one someday.

Four weeks later, he called his mama and told her how excited he was to be back in a plane, though he was quietly baffled that there was no follow-up on the training schedule. She sounded happy, but he knew she thought it was a mixed blessing and secretly wished they had shut down the entire program, like they had once threatened, and sent him home instead.

He wrote to JoAnn from Pensacola with a feeling that something was quite odd. She had last written in April, telling him of difficulties at home, and was upset that he had stopped writing to her. She'd been more upbeat the previous fall, when she was inspired by her new college and asked if he'd worn her badge. It was her parting words, *When will I see you again?* that grabbed Jim by the heart and held great hope. He punched the air for joy then walked on it for a week. He immediately responded with a second group photo and asked if she could send one too. Coyly, he shared a dream in which they were looking down on moonlit city lights from their own little plane. But he hadn't heard back in a long time. Now, he wrote that he desperately wanted to see her, but he wasn't allowed out. Nor could he wear her badge in uniform, though he kept it in a special place.

"Cadets, you are now Midshipmen, Fourth Class," their new owner, Lieutenant White, told them at their first meeting. "That means you are officers of the United States Navy." To Jim, that suddenly made the eighteen months of college seem like physical torture, all for Marino's entertainment.

The Pensacola barracks had the same bunks as USC, but in smaller quarters. Pale and sparse, the rooms could have been hospital wards in a previous life. First they got new khakis and black shoes (which they learned to polish again), then they practiced standing proud and arrow straight in their new tailored aviator whites; they lined up for every briefing.

But the Navy had also cloned a new yelling Marine for Pensacola, along with a fresh batch of pit-bull drill sergeants who unleashed a new torrent of taunts from a seemingly bottomless pit.

"What did I do to get stuck with you saps?" White yelled during their first physical training. "You pukes wouldn't make it into the Marine Corps! And I'm here to weed out the next batch of you who don't deserve the privilege of being here. I guarantee that some of you will wash out and some of you will run home when the pain becomes unbearable."

Jim had a sinking feeling that the physicals were about to get tougher as he packed away his personal clothes, which would not be seen again for at least the next four months in pre-flight. He didn't have the heart to send them home like the other cadets, for fear of making an ominous impression on his mama.

His eyes were barely open when the cadets ran to the obstacle course at dawn on the Monday of the second week. The chin-ups, sit-ups, and star jumps were only a warm-up, and not one of them made it through the minimum five minutes of step-ups that followed.

The next morning at dawn, they ran to the O-course again, just as they would run everywhere every day. Jim and Frank were paired up first and sent hopping through the tire trap, one foot at a time like five-year-olds. Jim wedged his right sneaker on the off, burning precious seconds near the starting line. Frank, seemingly as light as a feather, blew past him and shot up the ropes of a twelve-foot bulkhead, then waited unnecessarily at the crawl under on the other side, while Jim lost his grip on the climb. He pulled himself over the bulkhead on his third try.

Jim's eyelids were a little wider today, but he could have dozed off while he crawled in the sand under the low beams. The pair monkeyed their way over a horizontal ladder, but slipped off the log bridges so many times that they were given a pass, so as not to hold up the next batch. Frank didn't make it out of the maze—there was no exit, and he hadn't followed instructions to jump the last bar. The sand on the home stretch might as well have been molasses.

All done, Jim, Frank, and three other cadets were designated Sub-P.T. (Physical Training) and ordered to return every Saturday morning until their nearly five tardy minutes were compressed down to two minutes and fifty-five seconds—and twice, to graduate pre-flight. Jim couldn't imagine the two-twelve course record, especially after the daily grueling warm-up and five minutes of step-ups.

The next morning, simply walking anywhere seemed positively forbidden. The gym introduced the side horse, rope climb, parallel bars, and trampoline, after the morning of outdoor torture. Frank rocketed up the pigtail again, but he just couldn't vault the fake steed.

Soon the rope climb gave way to a parachute launch from a high platform. At first, Jim struggled to roll into the drop. His knees crunched with each landing and he scraped the floor mat every time he steadied himself to get up. If this was anything like the real thing, it seemed unnervingly close to hurtling to the ground without a harness at all.

Not long after that, they learned hand-to-hand combat. One cadet was blinded when Jim slammed him onto the mat during a takedown. Everyone had a nervous few hours until the man's sight miraculously returned.

They paired Frank with one of the bigger guys, Mike, and he just couldn't get out of a choke hold. He tried desperately to pull, punch, and jerk his way to freedom, then finally slapped his opponent's clamped right hand just as he was about to turn blue. The man's grip gave way automatically, but he was flat on his back on the mat in less than five seconds, though mightily relieved to be breathing again.

"Alright, you lowlifes, I want twenty laps around the field. Then I want to see you by the pool. You've had plenty of time to learn the drill. Now get moving!" White ordered.

The men gave a loud "Yes, sir!" and jogged off in their flight uniforms. Jim wondered what was going on—it had been over two years since he joined the cadets, and they seemed to have put more torture on the schedule instead of airplanes.

"Seventy-eight bucks a month," Frank enthused as they jogged the final stretch to the pool building. "I like this place already."

"Maybe enough to go home for a day or two," Jim said. "I just have to see JoAnn."

Jim knew they only allowed him one Sunday afternoon of freedom, and he had to be in his barracks by ten-thirty every night until he was done here. That meant staying put until the end of February. He looked ahead at the pool house. "But I can't go anywhere if I drown in the deep end first."

"You know what? I never learned to swim. I can't believe this is where I flunk out. I haven't even sat in the front of an airplane yet," Frank said.

"Relax. Just take a deep breath and hold it. You'll float. You'll be fine."

They arrived at the pool and stood in line by the water. A chief petty officer promised them it would not be like surfing lessons on the beach.

"We're going to teach you how to survive if you get shot out of the sky," White said, in a booming voice that echoed around the pool building. "Eight out of ten of you can expect to land on water at some point, in battle. If you ditch, you'll have to stay afloat in rough seas until you can be rescued. That could mean

63

hours in a nice warm soup if you're lucky. But you don't want the sun to burn your face off. Now, which of you gets seasick?"

The cadets stood quietly. No one said a thing.

"Okay, which of you cannot swim?"

Still, no one answered, though palpable fear showed on some of the craggy faces.

White rolled his eyes. "Right, you saps. In that case, all of you give me twenty laps in the water." He glanced at his watch. "The rest of you stay right where you are."

The cadets affirmed loudly, as most jumped into the pool, while a handful, including Frank, remained watching sheepishly from the side.

* * *

Several weeks later, Jim and Frank were already transmitting Morse code and learning to speed-read at nearly six hundred words per minute. Jim used it to grind through *The Foundations of Naval Power*. His head ached from relearning aircraft engines, which he'd practically forgotten since college.

The math and science classes stumped most of the cadets, though he was one of the few who could do motion, forces, and sound. But every hour of the thirty-six on electronics were painful. Atomic structure, electron theory, static and dynamic electricity, Ohm's law, and electromagnetic induction just didn't stay inside his head. They entered his ears and eyeballs, but nothing reached out to grab them before they passed out the other side.

Meanwhile, his O-course was down to three-thirty and tied with Frank's. One of the other three stragglers had already made good time. On the other hand, lumbering giant Mike, with limbs the size of King Kong's, simply couldn't overcome his massive inertia and move fast enough. Standing next to Frank, it was anyone's guess how he'd fit into a small fighter when the day came; maybe they'd allow him to stretch out his legs from the back of a two-seater.

Now, with the easy seconds already shaved off, the clock was already ticking on their exit test.

CHAPTER 10 - WATER

Early-February 1952

The new year arrived within eight weeks of their first splash in the pool. Jim and his fellow cadets—all of whom could now backstroke, breaststroke, sidestroke, and crawl, both dressed and undressed—moved on to water training in the real world. They were herded to the Bayou Grande inlet of Pensacola Bay and lined up against the waterline in flight suits to trial a brand new form of terror. A small army of CPOs stood guard, and frogmen were already in the water.

The obligatory yelling began. "Okay, you pukes. You just fell out of the sky, and the enemy is firing at you. Firing their cannons at you. Shooting to kill you. But your plane is in the soup, pulling you down, sucking you into the deep. Fifteen feet down. You catch my drift?" White looked along the line. "I want all of you down there now. Down to the bottom. You got it?" He held a stopwatch, pressed the trigger, and hollered, "Go! Go! Go!"

The line leaped into the water. Jim first ducked at the edge and searched for the murky bottom. Clutching his breath, he dived in and plunged into the icy depths. His head and eyes throbbed. He looked around for Frank, but all he could see was a mass of ghostly silhouettes thrusting in all directions, while eerily hovering frogmen, who shifted in and out of focus, kept watch.

Not too soon, seaweed wafted against his hands. He was sure he must be near the bottom. He reached out for it, wondering if he'd gone far enough. A diver pointed further down. Jim's lungs felt like they could explode, but he couldn't tell where the water ended. He pushed on, tipped the bottom, and torpedoed back to the shimmering light of day.

He broke the surface with a big gulp of air to ease his aching chest and wondered if he'd made it look too easy when White came around and leaned over him with a piercing stare that looked like trouble.

The man stood up straight and launched another tirade instead of just talking. "Okay, you, you, you, and you ..." Jim was one of them, though not Frank, "I want a mile out of you. Go! The fight's not over. You boys aren't home yet, sleeping in your cozy bunks. That nice warm bath you want is on the other side, over there. You're going to freeze and die in the next three minutes if you don't move it. You're still at sea. Now go! Go! Go!"

Jim and three others swam along the shore to a creek with an oil slick line on the surface. The officers lit some Texas Tea while the men lined up behind a diving platform. Jim jumped into the water first, heaving his legs back down to fifteen feet underwater. He touched a frogman near the bottom, looked up at the orange glow of fire, on the water's surface, and passed under the smoldering slick to the other side. White later assured him the next time he did that, it would be for real, alone, and in the middle of a shark-infested ocean somewhere a million miles from home.

Jim crawled out of the waves and collapsed onto a rocky ledge. Water dripped from every crevice of his flight suit. For a moment, he wondered what he'd gotten himself into. He'd joined the Navy to fly planes, yet he'd spent more time drenched than in the previous twenty years. And he had not yet logged a single flight hour. Was it all a ruse? Did the Navy not need pilots?

That same afternoon, after a stubborn three-twenty on the O-course that nearly broke him, Jim finally imagined the smell of avgas.

A short-sleeved professor in a thin black tie and glasses, stood in front of his new class. "Okay, we're going to start with a textbook called *Aerodynamics for Naval Aviators.*"

Jim listened from the back row, still barely dry from the morning.

"Some of you studied the principles of flight in college. Right? That's lift, drag, thrust, and so on?" He looked around the room for acknowledgment, but the faces looked exhausted. "Basic stuff, right?"

Simple indeed, but no one had the energy to answer. Several cadets shifted uncomfortably in their seats at the sight of a new tome on the table in front of them.

"Okay, please turn to the contents of your books," said the professor.

Jim opened the hardcover and thumbed through the pages, seeing margin to margin and cover to cover technical properties of flight and the atmosphere. He turned back to the contents and glanced at the main headings, labeled: *Bernoulli's Principle, Aerodynamic Forces, Lift Conditions and Devices, Aerodynamic Pitching, Friction, and Induced Drag.* The contents alone spanned another ten pages. He paused and sighed softly, then flipped through the book again and scanned the tiny footnotes which were crammed into every available space. The whole room could have groaned for a nap after the morning's swim.

"Okay, we're going to start with atmospheric properties. You'll need to understand the behavior of airflow and various aerodynamic forces for good, precise flying," the professor said. He looked ready to plunge tongue-first into his domain.

He wrote an equation on the blackboard. It was for *altitude pressure ratio.* Jim scanned the book and saw that it was equivalent to something called *ambient static pressure* divided by *standard sea level static pressure.* It came with new scientific symbols he'd never seen before.

"Okay, who can tell me what static pressure is?" the professor asked.

When no one said a word, he launched a verbal attack. "Well, the static pressure at any height is the result of the mass of air supported above that height." He paused to look around, then continued like a robot on program. "At standard sea level, the static pressure of air is fourteen-point-seven psi." He scanned the cadets eyes for lightbulbs, but the power was clearly out.

Jim looked down at his book again. The question was answered right there on the page, but the information flowed into his eyeballs and straight out of his ear holes as he read it. Next to him, another cadet twirled a pen in his hand as he stared blankly at a diagram on the next page.

Over the next hour, the professor added temperature ratio equations and summarized density ratio and kinematic viscosity. He introduced the standard altitude table, the dreaded Bernoulli equation (which Jim had seen before), airflow and pressure variations in a tube, various measures of airspeed,

69

pitot-static systems, airspeed compressibility corrections (at various calibrated airspeeds), and density altitude charts. He promised them the next lesson would cover the coefficient of lift with different flap configurations at different angles of attack.

It amazed Jim, as he sat in the back, that up to that point there had been nothing as simple as turning a key, starting an airplane engine, and just taking off. Instead, a whole new language was staring back at him for things he never knew existed. He felt like he'd have to grow a whole new brain just to store it all for the tests that were surely coming their way.

* * *

March 1952

The cadets began the final phase of training to bail out of a crippled airplane over water. Jim lost count of the number of times they dragged him across the bay with a parachute line to simulate a windy landing in rough seas, even though the Gulf of Mexico bay didn't have ten-foot waves like the open ocean. Nevertheless, they were reassured that the parachutes came guaranteed with a free replacement for any that failed to deploy in the air.

White separated ten cadets from a group of fifteen standing by the pool in Training Tank One. "I want eight of you in the water! Now!"

As they jumped in, Jim and Frank remained stunned, at the edge, replaying transgressions in their heads to see if they'd been rumbled for something.

"God is smiling down on you two today," White said. They looked confused. "Those eight of your buddies will land in the water at sometime during combat."

Jim and Frank felt unexpectedly relieved.

"You!" White pointed to a cadet in the water. "Out!"

The man hauled himself from the pool.

"It's your lucky day too, buddy," White said. "But those seven will be dead in three minutes. Drown or freeze; either way, it's over for them. On a normal day, you'd be in there too, in your own upturned airplane."

The cadets looked on in horror as White introduced their savior, the infamous Dilbert Dunker—a fiery red roll cage, up a two-track ramp into the water. It resembled the cockpit of an airplane, cut off at the front and back.

The first cadet to take the plunge made a terrific splash in the machine and drenched the spectators, who held their own breaths until he resurfaced again.

The contraption was winched back up to launch height as Jim, next in line, poured out and pulled on a pair of shared sneakers, a cold wet shirt, and dripping pants over his swim trunks, from the last guy.

He grabbed a parachute pack and climbed the steps to a twenty-foot ramp over the pool, wondering just where to put it.

"Under your butt. There's a block of wood in there," said the boatswain's mate at the top.

Jim placed it on the seat then hopped in and tightened his straps. He glanced around at the heavy padding which covered every strut, fearing that it did not promise a smooth ride.

"Keep your right hand on the stick, and hold your left arm in front of your face," advised the boatswain's mate. He checked Jim's harness, gave a thumbs-up, then pressed a buzzer.

Without warning, a latch released the device and Jim plunged down the chute, cutting the water at a forty-five degree angle in under a second. The Dunker flipped upside down in a cloud of bubbles five feet below.

He was stunned and froze, floating inverted and holding his breath as he tried to compute which way was up. A few seconds later, he unbuckled his harness, remembering that he had to get out as the water cleared again. He grabbed the windshield, pulled down hard, shot out of the seat, and bolted back to the surface, fearing a watery grave.

His nostrils ached from flooding, and his stomach churned as he stripped for the next cadet at the pool's edge.

He'd just taken off the second shoe when White said, "Go again, Cobb."

Jim looked up. He couldn't imagine having to do that twice. He'd already survived the pretend ditching. "But, sir, you only ditch once." He regretted the words as soon as he said them. Damn it, he thought. Fatigue and exhaustion, or the water, had loosened his jaw a bit too much.

White seethed quietly. "I'll see you go again, Cobb," he demanded.

Jim looked down at his soaked clothes and sighed. His whole body was sore and his head was full of water.

"Which half of *go again*, don't you get, Cobb?"

Jim picked up a dripping wet shoe and stuffed a squelching foot inside. He shivered in the ice-cold clothes as he walked like a stiff board around the pool and up the steps to the Dunker again.

His second turn was much like the first, except this time he held his nose before plunging into the depths. But failing to hold his left hand in front of his face as advised, the water gave him a sharp slap on the right cheek as he hit the surface.

He unbuckled more quickly and bolted to freedom again.

Fortunately, White signaled for him to return to the line, though he also sent the next cadet back to the creek for ocean training after he chickened out of the exercise altogether.

Frank had been too slow to escape the submerged cockpit and received a thumbs down from the divers after they helped him out. He did it again. And again. And again, each time receiving a drenched disapproval. Looking thoroughly washed out, he too rejoined the line after his fourth ride.

White dismissed the cadets at the end of the day, except for Jim and Frank.

Frank went two more times, but each time he was denied attainment. He had only just learned to swim and never looked so desperate.

"Are you going for your first record today, Baum?" teased White.

After Frank's sixth dunk, Jim donned the wet clothes for his third attempt. They submerged him a fourth time, and a fifth time, then he got back in line when Frank went up for his seventh try. Frank had figured out how to unbuckle, but just couldn't tell which way was up fast enough. It seemed like a miracle to Jim that he was still in the water at all.

Frank groaned miserably and almost fell back into the pool as he got out and undressed. Jim held him up as he took off a sneaker and poured it out.

"Cobb, you're dismissed."

Jim reached for the shoe as it slipped from Frank's hand.

"What are you still doing here, Cobb? I said dismissed!"

"Frank just needs a hand here," Jim said innocently.

"Cobb, you have to listen to instructions when they are given! I'll see you on the O-course tomorrow at six sharp so we can get some practice."

73

* * *

Frank limped back to the barracks that night. "I can't believe it. Did you see that?"

"What?" asked Jim, his head buried in aerodynamics home-work under a lamplight on his bunk.

"The sign outside." Frank groaned stiffly, as he rolled onto his mattress under Jim's. "Oh God, I feel like I've swallowed half the pool," he grumbled. "Twelve rides in that thing. They're trying to keep us out of the air. I know it. They must save money by keeping their planes on the ground and dumping us in that pool instead. I should have joined an airline. Maybe this will all be a bad dream when I wake up."

Jim crept to the door in the dim light. Taped to it, in large letters, was a horizontal banner that read: *Never Again Volunteer Yourself.*

"Marines?" he whispered, scanning the courtyard.

But Frank didn't answer.

Jim returned to his bunk and glanced over the side when he heard nothing from below. Frank had already left the day behind—without setting any records; he remained well off the pace on the O-course and just two short of the trophy fourteen sorties in the Dilbert Dunker.

Jim closed his textbook, leaned back against his pillow, and flattened a piece of paper on a tome he was resting on his knee. Pausing to consider what to say, he wrote today's date at the top, then *JoAnn* underneath. The pen hovered over the page, and despite several letters of practice already under his belt, he wondered, as usual, how to begin. The tip dropped, and he told of his daily dunking, though still nothing to speak of above the water. For that, he was sure his mama would be pleased. He wrote how he would describe flying to the enemy, bore them to death with physics, then swim to safety. He explained how the yelling continued, as if they had just rolled the latest lieutenant off the assembly line with the standard issue voice box. P.S. Was she about to graduate from college or was there another year to go? He said he hoped to visit home when he got leave, and asked if she'd gotten his last few letters. He hadn't heard from her in almost a year, and he missed her.

CHAPTER 11 - HALF PAST THE HOUR

The next day

The following day brightened just before Jim staggered out onto the O-course alone. The sun hadn't quite broken the horizon, and with only a few hours' sleep, the morning chill penetrated deep inside his aching bones.

He waited for White in the dawn breeze, then waited some more. It seemed like thirty minutes had passed when White finally appeared, wiping the corner of his mouth as if he'd just enjoyed a hearty breakfast.

"What are you waiting for, Cobb? Get going, boy," White yelled, with his stopwatch in hand before he'd even arrived at the starting line.

Jim was quietly angry at the frigid delay, but held it in. He stumbled through the tires with stiff muscles. His calves, arms and back suffered with every step around the course to the finish line.

"Just where do you think you are, Cobb? Three-minutes-thirty is just not worthy of our time and attention here. What in the world did you get me out of bed for?"

Jim was stunned. It was White who had given the orders. But he had slipped backwards and returned with one of the worst times he had ever done.

"What have you forgotten, Cobb? Did they teach you anything in that college of yours?"

Jim looked at White blankly, then dropped to the ground and stretched out the pins in his hamstrings.

"You didn't warm up, did you, Cobb? Have you forgotten everything? Are you even awake this morning?"

Jim felt furious—White was right. He could have kicked himself if his brain was working well enough to coordinate his stiff, dead legs.

"You haven't learned a damn thing here, have you, Cobb? Why are we being told to waste our time on you?"

Jim felt humiliated.

"On your back, boy."

Jim did as instructed.

"Let's start with a hundred sit-ups. We need to get the wheels turning here or this is going nowhere fast."

Jim began the fierce struggle, thinking he couldn't have picked a worse time to fail. He was no morning lark. He could stay up all night, but now his body simply refused to warm up.

Jim battled past fifty, slogged to seventy, and ground out the remaining thirty.

He lay back in the sand to catch his breath, but White yelled in his face. "On your hands and knees, Cobb! This ain't your bed. I want a hundred push-ups out of you."

Jim was terrified as he turned and pumped furiously. He hadn't done a hundred yet and was sure he wouldn't make even two-thirds.

His triceps were already screaming at thirty-five. He was on the verge of collapsing at fifty, then finally lost count at seventy. He dropped, exhausted, face-first into the sand moments later.

White looked down at him as if he'd just squashed a bug under his shoe. "You're not cut out for this, Cobb. Do you think this is a vacation or something? I would not have you in my company like this."

He walked away, saying, "Six a.m., Cobb. You'd better make it good, or you'll be packing and on the first train home. There's one at half past every hour."

Jim remained face-down and panting in the sand. "O'course, sir."

* * *

The next morning, he got up thirty minutes early to stretch while waiting for White again. He couldn't screw up a second time, even though his aching body had robbed him of another good night's sleep. Fortunately, the newfound adrenaline had chased away the morning chill.

White showed up at a quarter after six and, without conversation, sent Jim running around the hurdles again.

"You been up all night practicing out here, Cobb?" sneered White, as Jim sprinted to the finish line. "Three-ten? Is that really you, Cobb?" He studied his stopwatch and suggested that it was faulty. "Maybe I need to get a new one here. Go again."

He pulled a long-folded journal from his back pocket, leaned against a sidebar, and bowed his head to read as Jim began. White glanced at his watch occasionally, but never once looked up at Jim's progress.

Three minutes and five seconds later, Jim felt every agonizing step around the track, though he knew he'd still come up short.

The mandatory hundred sit-ups followed. Jim's abs throbbed with each contraction and threatened to lock up at about ninety.

78

Still, determined not to give White the satisfaction of a white towel, he made not a gripe in protest. Over and over, he folded and straightened without a sound escaping his lips, though the pain increased with every crunch.

He turned to face the sand, afraid that his arms would give way with only a handful of push-ups done. If he dropped now, he might not get up again. Still, he said nothing and slogged his way to seventy.

White was indifferent when Jim collapsed to the ground soon after.

"I think another morning in the pool would do you some good, Cobb. Six a.m."

White walked away.

Jim lay there relieved, thinking maybe the trains weren't running today.

* * *

The next morning it looked like White had gone insane. He demanded two hundred laps of the pool, which was just as well, since it was the first morning in a week with rain outside.

Jim's front crawl was sloppy all the way, and he could barely pull himself out of the water when he had finished.

He lay sprawled on the floor at the edge of the pool.

"Get up, Cobb."

Jim felt like he was going to throw up on White's feet if he moved another muscle. That would be the ultimate embarrassment and surely seal his fate. Still, he said nothing.

"I said get up, Cobb. Did you hear me? You're not catching a damn thing, are you? By God, we have so much work to do."

That was all Jim needed to hear. The nausea subsided for a

moment. He would not be getting on a train today. He had to pull through. Jim staggered to his feet and threw up in the men's room when White was gone.

* * *

Jim, Frank, and Max trudged across the yard through the rain to their barracks right after dinner that night.

"Complain about it," Max urged, after Jim had shared the details of his special dawn classes with White each day.

"No," Jim said flatly, "I'm not going to give him the satisfaction."

"He can't keep doing this," Frank said. "You didn't come here to be tortured like this. Who does he think he is?"

The trio froze as White walked up behind them. Several cadets jumped to their feet at their bunks.

White's eyes narrowed as he looked around the room, then walked over to Jim's bunk. "This yours, Cobb?"

Jim said nothing from the door as White inspected his bed, shoes, and uniform, which hung in a tall, single open closet.

"What's this mess?" White pointed to a pile of papers at Jim's bedside.

Jim replied that they were letters from family—some from JoAnn and a few from his mama. JoAnn's and his father's special badges were beside them.

"Let me get something straight. You'll keep your bunk tidy, midshipman. This here's a fire hazard." White picked them up and threw them across Jim's bunk.

The other cadets held their breath.

Jim was furious and no longer cared what happened next. "Sir, those are—"

"Midshipmen don't talk back to a superior officer in my class." White looked as if someone had slapped him across the face. "In fact, I think I'm finally done with you, Cobb. I want you outside now."

White marched Jim back out into the rain while he stood under cover in the doorway. Another group of cadets slowed in the courtyard as they arrived from dinner and slipped sheepishly past him into the building.

"On your hands and knees, Cobb. You know the drill."

The cadets watched from their windows and from the doorway behind White as Jim got down on all fours in a puddle of mud. He knew he had no chance after just eating; he still hadn't managed a hundred push-ups. His shoulders were sore from the morning swim, and he'd been feverish all day.

White watched triumphantly as Jim spread his hands in the dirt and began to press. He took out a fold of paper from a coat pocket and read it again.

At about forty, White yelled through the rain. "Give up now, Cobb. It's time to go home. Your buddies in the field can't count on you. This isn't your game. The O-course has beaten you, Cobb. Why bother? It's too tiresome to watch." White turned and looked at a dozen cadets, gaping, wide-eyed, in the windows.

Jim continued, feeling as if he might drown in the deluge at any moment. His mind went back to boot camp, and he thought there was no cutlery training in the world that could help him now. Well pressed suits and shiny boots seemed like some kind of child's play.

"Say the word, Cobb, and you're out of here. Remember—half past the hour." White looked up supremely at the audience.

Still, Jim went on. He felt dizzy as he passed seventy. He

gasped for air as streams of rain trickled down his lips. Something in the mud dug into his right hand, but he knew it would be a crushing defeat if he stopped or lost his rhythm now. A spasm shot across his right chest and under the crease of his arm. Still, he continued. He'd lost count. He had no idea how this was going to end.

Jim paused for a moment to ease the pain at the top of the thrust.

"Well, if that's really the best you can do," White said, leaning against a doorpost. "I can't wait here for all this again." He stood up straight, scanned the sky, and skipped across the wet courtyard with a folded paper over his head to catch the rain.

Jim grimaced in anger, watching White's boots pass by out of the corner of his eye. "Coward," he muttered.

He would do a hundred, White or no White. He guessed he was at eighty and pushed on. His right hand stung under the mud. He was swimming in the rain. Ninety-five. He would make it. One hundred. He screamed as he held on for a second, then slowly lowered himself and pushed back up with everything he had.

He fell face-first into the dirt. The pain in his right hand eased. His muscles relaxed, and a moment later he was on his hands and knees, turning to see White disappear into another building thirty yards away.

Dripping, and caked in mud, he staggered to his feet and looked at the stunned silence staring back at him from inside the barracks.

He looked down at a piercing pain at the bottom of his right hand and saw blood seeping into the dripping mulch around his fingers.

* * *

The next day, the torrent of torture had all but destroyed his rib cage by the time he made his third parachute jump from the ledge. He'd done a hundred and one push-ups for an audience the night before, but it had come at a price. Now, still prone on the landing mat in front of the class, he reeled in agony, unable to stand as his abs locked up in a sharp spasm. Frank and Max hauled him off the gym floor, both secretly soothing their own waistlines after the morning workout, along with every other cadet in class.

* * *

Sixteen weeks into pre-flight, Jim was still in the game, and it was time for White's last hurrah.

When he arrived at the O-course for his exit test, he was still recovering from three nights in the woods and swamps of the Eglin Reservation with the Navy's Pre-Flight Survival Unit.

After scavenging for wood to build a fire, he had caught only a handful of striped smallmouth bass and a bluegill panfish for dinner, despite setting traps and snares each night.

But it was the upturned life raft for a bed that locked up his lower back. Only a splayed parachute in the trees above diverted the night's rain. He was in agony with new blisters at the end of a fifteen-mile hike on the final day.

Now, the next morning, he and his fellow cadets would have to run the O-course twice, in time, or all the torture would have been for naught.

They all managed the first five minutes of step-ups, though Mike Sanders, sweating profusely and puffing like a steam train, nearly fell over his own feet at four and a half.

Several dead certs went around the O-course ahead of the obvious laggards. Jim, Frank, and a few others waited in line and watched the aces high-five their way to basic flight training before the "slackers" had even started.

Jim was paired with Max and ran the course like a hound after a rabbit.

White stared at his stopwatch, looking grimly satisfied when Jim crossed the finish line. "In two minutes, Cobb, I want to see that again."

Jim didn't dare open his mouth in case White changed his mind or called for another round of torture. But it made little sense. Why was White looking pleased? Was he out?

Max was less than a meter behind, and he had to repeat it as well.

White paired Frank and Mike last, by which time the successful members of the brotherhood had already returned to their barracks. Only Jim and Max remained to cheer on the final pair.

Frank shot up the ropes at the high bulkhead, as Mike, the giant, struggled to pull himself up. He paused there, burning precious seconds to catch his breath.

Frank slithered feverishly through the crawl under, his eyes fixed on his goal as he raced over the low bulkhead, skipped over the logs, and shot through the maze. He flew across the sand and collapsed, breathless, under the finish sign.

White looked vindicated when Mike crossed the line fifteen seconds later. "Sanders. Back to your barracks. Three-thirty-five ain't gonna cut it. This ain't the holidays, in case you haven't noticed!"

"No, sir," Mike protested angrily. "I'll do it again."

White glared at him, and Jim thought he was going to attack

Mike. "Get back to your barracks now, Sanders."

"Sir, I'll do it again. I can do it; I know I can."

White's eyes narrowed in his usual way. "Sanders! You heard me."

"I'm ready, sir. This is it."

White looked stunned for a moment. He ordered Mike to stand back, then looked down at Frank, who was still in the sand, panting like a Labrador. "Baum, are you done sunning yourself? On your feet. Cobb, you too."

Mike parked himself next to Max and doubled over, dripping with sweat and out of breath.

Frank shot to his feet, lined up with Jim, and got White's go.

He looked positively consumed as he fled the starting line, a hair's breadth ahead of Jim. He was up the ropes by the time Jim finished dancing across the tires like someone had stuffed them with fresh hot coals.

Jim leaped up the bulkhead and almost caught Frank as they snaked through the crawl under together.

They were neck-and-neck at the horizontal bars, but Jim, in his frenzy, lost his grip, fell, cursed, and bounced right back up again.

Frank nearly tumbled off the log bridge, but Jim shot out a steadying right hand to catch him, just as White's head was down.

He gave way at the entrance to the maze, knowing that Frank's smaller frame would be faster. They shimmied through, hurdled the last bar, and sped across the sand on the home stretch.

White's eyes glowed subtly, as if he had just stepped out into a warm, sunny morning after winter. He slowly turned his head in Jim's direction and said, "To your barracks, both of you."

Jim could hardly believe it. Did he just hear that he was

85

finished? That White was history? No train home? No more persecution?

About to ask for their times, Frank leaned toward White's stopwatch. Jim shushed him and pulled him back, figuring they'd better let sleeping dogs lie. But instead of leaving as ordered, they waited quietly in line as Mike and Max lined up for their final push.

White rolled his eyes, grunted, and set the last pair in motion.

Max flew over the tires, shot up the ropes, and tumbled down the other side of the bulkhead before Mike was even out of the tire trap.

He slithered through the crawl under and skipped over the logs as Mike lost his grip on the bulkhead ropes. He jumped up, grabbed and pulled with everything he had.

Jim couldn't hold back from the sideline. "Come on, Mike! Go on! Go!"

White turned and sneered at him.

Max had already charged over the monkey bars.

Jim glanced sideways at White's stopwatch and saw that Max might just make it.

"Go Max! Go!"

"Cobb! Baum! Why aren't you in your barracks like I said?" yelled White.

Max shot through the maze, hurled himself over the last bar, and tripped on his butt. He got to his feet and dashed across the sand like a missile, landing feet first in a skid across the line.

Gasping for air, he stared up at White, who, against his better judgment, looked impressed.

Jim saw an astonishing two minutes and thirty-five seconds on White's watch. It was the fastest time he'd ever seen.

But White ignored them all as a new resignation grew on his

face.

Mike had stopped at the entrance to the maze, his mouth contorted with pain. One hand was down, gripping his right hamstring. Head down, he rubbed it hard, then looked up at the finish sign.

Max was still lying in the sand, staring at Mike, and seemed to have almost stopped breathing.

Jim was about to run out when Mike limped into the maze, still clutching his leg.

White's face fell as Mike stumbled left and right through the maze, ducking under the last beam, and shuffled across the sand to the finish line.

White turned to him as he limped quietly past the crowd toward the barracks, neither stopping nor turning back.

Jim was sure that an ocean breeze had given him a tailwind on the O-course when he returned to the barracks that morning— he and Frank had survived the pre-flight ordeal and had made two-forty-eight and two-fifty-three on their final run.

CHAPTER 12 - PUKE

March 1952, Saufley Field near Pensacola, Florida

Jim and Frank's final O-course times were worthy enough to earn Midshipman Third Class, and jettison White, though he remained a strange enigma in Jim's mind.

They'd been trained to protect the Navy's investment. Now it promised to spend. The flying finally began at Naval Air Station Saufley Field near Pensacola, almost immediately after Frank lamented its absence.

The first night, Jim dragged Frank back to his bunk after one too many beers following two years of sobriety. The next day, wearing new brown shoes, and greens with anchors on their collars, they met Squadron Leader May.

First, he presented the silver, all-metal North American SNJ-4 at the assignment board where each lesson began. With a single prop, it bore a large American star on its body and a US Navy emblem painted just forward of the rear elevator and on each wing. To Jim, the cockpit resembled a small prison cell, with its protruding glass canopy crisscrossed with dark bars between small, equally squared panes.

Jim had learned to locate every control blindfolded by the end of the first week when they joined Basic Training Group 2 at nearby Whiting North.

And after four weeks, thanks to his previous experience, he'd already mastered the basics of flying. Surprised, the instructor asked if he'd done this before. "A little," he said, holding the fact that he had a license, though it must have expired by now.

He was well ahead of the group when the infamous aerobatics training began on a warm April morning. A steady stream of SNJs went up and down as he walked toward his plane. It had just taxied onto the ramp, but the cadet remained inside, searching the cabin as he unbuckled.

He saw a yellow sheet on the canopy as the instructor emerged from the back seat and conferred with his own. "This one's out. The kid threw up out the window and got it all back in the face. I told him not to open it. He's mopping up right now."

Jim and his instructor took the next SNJ to pull up. They checked it over. He put on a green cloth cap, stowed his parachute, jumped into the front seat, and strapped himself into the light green cocoon. He pulled the canopy forward while the instructor installed himself in the back.

Smoke billowed from the exhaust as the engine fired. The plane captain gave the all clear, and the instructor guided them straight to the runway. Minutes later, the tail wheel came up and they were cruising over Florida.

At five thousand feet, the instructor looped and spun the plane to show an elated Jim what was to be done. "Here's what I want you to do," he said. "I'm going to roll the plane first, then push the nose up. We're going into an inverted spin. I want you to put your hands on top of your head and keep them there at all times. You got that?"

"Sure," said Jim, grinning from ear-to-ear and eager to make an impression—after all, he'd played around a lot in the old crop duster.

The instructor duly rolled the plane, then flipped it and rolled it again in under ten seconds. He continued to roll it over and over, swinging Jim around his small space and hanging him by the straps whenever he was upside down. Jim expected to fall out of his seat and crash through the glass. His hands flailed uncontrollably in front of his eyes whenever he put them on his head. The instructor continued with Immelmann turns, skidding the plane sideways before dropping it in the opposite direction.

Five minutes later, feeling a satisfied grin beaming at the back of his head, Jim lost it and puked into a sick bag. It was the first time he'd thrown up on an airplane.

Although he felt like a rookie, he mustered up some fortitude and asked to try it again.

"Remember, you can stay upside down as long as you like if you stay at idle power, then wait for the oil pressure to rise before adding power when you're right-side up."

To Jim, that didn't sound as plainly obvious as it was ejected.

He took the controls and tried a slow roll, then a snap roll. But his bravado just brought forth more puke. He struggled to stow his sick bag where it wouldn't buzz or spill.

The instructor asked calmly, "Ready for some falling leaves?"

Jim retched again and quickly refused.

"Okay," the instructor said. "First lesson. As demonstrated, young pukes may want to skip breakfast while doing aerobatics." He let the experience sink in. "I think we're done here for today." He slid the plane through the air and, to Jim's relief, turned back to base.

But Jim's big moment came soon after. He'd flown many hours in daylight (along with several rounds of aerobatics) when his instructor finally uttered the immortal words, on his way to another plane one morning, "She's yours now, Jim, but please bring her back in one piece! Practice those aerobatics and make sure a dive earthward doesn't occur, so that flight pay continues to be paid. You got that?"

Elated, Jim threw his soft cap into the air. He'd finally soloed. The other cadets snipped his tie that afternoon as he advanced to Midshipman Second Class.

* * *

Keep a straight head when entering a spin and look around, observing other pilots and the wind direction, the instructor had written on Jim's check sheet. *Will need to perfect his Section C aerobatics if he wants to graduate and land on a carrier some day,* he had added.

Jim went at it like a battering ram, practicing solo for hours. But the falling leaves continued to bring out the worst in him. His stomach just wouldn't settle, and it fed a new anxiety that grew with every practice. He grabbed a handful of toilet paper rolls to mop up the vomit, but struggled to keep the plane clean. Meanwhile, the others were making it look easy and not giving anything away, so he kept his difficulties to himself too.

On his twentieth attempt, a roll of paper slipped from his hand while he was wiping his mouth. The canopy was open. It tumbled out and unraveled as it fell from five thousand feet. A long vertical streamer now hung in the air. He cursed, still feeling sick. He had to clear the air for the other pilots, so he pushed the throttle for a coordinated turn and came back at the streamer, thinking he'd catch the line and pull it back in. It was one of his fastest turns, but the plane just shot through the vertical line, only cutting off the bottom tenth with its propeller.

He was alarmed as the long tail continued to grow and waft north toward the city. He slid the plane in the air and aimed for the bottom third. The wind pushed the streamer to the left and he missed it completely. The tube had fully unwound. He looked around for other planes and reluctantly pressed his microphone. He had to warn them.

Without saying a word, he let go of the microphone, figuring he'd never hear the end of it. He had to take it down quickly. He pulled an Immelmann and came back as fast as he dared, slashing through the top half with his left wing. After pushing the plane into a roll, he pulled another sideways skid and sliced the streamer twice while inverted, then dived vertically down the remainder and leveled into it, leaving only a small portion for the ground.

Twenty minutes later, adrenaline was still pumping through his body as he landed at Whiting North with only vapor in his tanks. He walked into the briefing room without another hint of nausea or talk of streamers.

After that, he made rapid, churn-free progress in aerobatics — and the cadets noticed. He shared his new training hack with the class, and within a week it was impossible to relieve himself anywhere on the base. The cadets had dropped the entire supply of toilet paper on southern Florida.

The following week, May marched Jim and his buddies outside in the rain to face the base commander, and they each received two hundred push-ups and two weeks of cleanup duty around town.

* * *

The cadets moved to South Whiting and managed to fly in formation without hitting each other. But the dreaded night solo was a whole new experience for Jim. Unable to see anything, he could have sworn he was flying upside down or sideways for several miles on a dreary night over the Gulf of Mexico without even knowing it.

Then, after dinner one night, they lined up for a government educational film. Although it was aimed mainly at schoolchildren, Jim and his class were also shown it, in case they were called upon to provide public security in the event of a Red attack.

"Gentlemen, it's a short film. Only ten minutes," May said, shuttering the windows while a reel-to-reel projector whirred in the back of the room.

"Duck and cover, duck and cover," sang a cartoon ensemble on screen. A monkey's cracker exploded and a nearby turtle dived into its shell.

The narrator, Robert Middleton, seemed oddly calm about the horror. "Now, there's a new danger, children. An atomic bomb could explode at any time, with or without warning."

Jim saw faces fall around him in the flickering light of the screen. His pulse raced as enemy planes appeared on film, pretending to drop bombs on ordinary Americans. Families ducked for cover. The room chuckled softly as a couple covered their heads with a picnic blanket and squirmed underneath, their elbows and knees flailing in all directions. Another family rolled down their sleeves to protect their arms from radiation exposure.

Middleton continued matter-of-factly. "The scalding is worse than the worst sunburn."

The cheers died away instantly.

Jim imagined a school bus, the streets, and all the picnics in the park wiped out by a massive explosion. He looked up at the shuttered windows and wished he could roll down his own sleeves, though he had none today.

"So, class, what are you supposed to do when you see the flash?" asked the turtle.

"Duck and cover," the kids in the movie screamed back.

The ensemble looped again. "Duck and cover, duck and cover."

Jim's mind raced as he imagined the Reds rounding up children, packing them up, and shipping them off to have their brains wiped. He wondered if people who were bundled over simply died on the spot. Nowhere seemed safe from such devastation. He thought of the terrible toll on Hiroshima and Nagasaki, and of Truman's new threat to drop the bomb on North Korea.

"My uncle said the Reds talk to UFOs." It was another cadet who chuckled softly and leaned in to whisper in Jim's ear. "He said *they have radiation beams in the sky. They'll shoot you down if they find you up there in that plane of yours again.*"

Atomic bombs loomed large in Jim's mind that night. He remembered his father and wrote to JoAnn and his mama, urging them both to find a safe place in case the worst really happened.

It also occurred to him not to be so fatalistic, or the threat would rob him of his own life. Maybe a life with JoAnn. They could just pick up where they'd left off. He trusted her and felt comfortable with her. How could she say no? He'd be done soon and they'd be at a wonderful age to get married. He could do that. JoAnn felt like an oasis in his world, which suddenly seemed to be all about death and destruction.

* * *

Late 1952, Saufley Field, Florida

In late summer, Jim and Frank returned to Basic Training Group 5 at Saufley Field, where they had first started flying.

Jim shot through gunnery with the help of a new Navy aviation training film in which Ensign Dilbert loaded his wing guns with bullets. "Don't be a Dilbert. Beware of propellers and don't kill your friends," he advised after firing a round of ammunition at civilians. One of his finer suggestions during formation flying was, "Don't mow down buddies while searching for and spraying targets." It all seemed very sensible to Jim, and he put it into practice right away.

He learned to stall, fall gracefully out of the air, and land on a tiny strip no bigger than the deck of an aircraft carrier during Field Carrier Landing Practice at nearby Bronson Field.

One October morning, the instructor said. "I got my wings on the Saipan. Looks like you'll find yours on the Cabot."

Jim had just heard the sign-off for the Carrier Qualification. The CQ was the ultimate test. If he passed, he'd finally become the pilot of his dreams. If he failed, three years of hard work and physical torture would land him right back at a farm.

"Now all you have to do is land your plane on a deck in the sea several times without hitting the boat, running off the side, or falling into the water," the instructor said. "If you fall in, it's cold enough to kill you before they can fish you out. Think you can handle that?"

CHAPTER 13 - TRAPS

October 1952, Pensacola, Florida

One bright morning a week later, Jim was back in Pensacola, where he'd already learned to swallow copious amounts of water. He was scheduled for a carrier check flight on the USS Cabot in the Gulf of Mexico.

He glanced down at Frank's bunk when he woke up that morning and saw that it lay untouched.

"Any word?" he asked Max on his way to the breakfast mess. "He's been out all night."

"I heard he went home. Said he wanted to tell his family about the CQ."

"Oh, he didn't mention it. Wasn't he out flying last night? I'm sure he was on a night run."

"Probably stranded somewhere if he was. Did you see the storm?"

"Yeah. I hope he's okay. Plus, he's going to miss the boat, literally, if he doesn't walk his ass back through that door pronto."

They entered the Pensacola dining room and sat down at a table, each with a breakfast tray in hand.

"I'm sure he can join the guys who are flying right out without stopping at the dock. They don't leave till afternoon," Max said.

"That's not on the schedule for today," another cadet replied.

They were sitting quietly, eating and thinking about the day's events, when an officer approached them. He, too, held a tray and stopped at their table. After a moment's pause, and looking rather pained, he said, "Word is that Frank Baum went down last night. Have you heard anything?"

Jim stopped chewing. "What do you mean?"

"They found his plane ten miles off course somewhere near Mobile, Alabama. Apparently he hit the thunderhead last night, and ..." The officer shrugged.

"Is he okay? Where is he?"

The officer shook his head, paused again, then said, "I'm sorry. I think there's going to be an announcement."

Jim and the seated cadets stopped eating as the man turned and sat with another group, telling them the news.

He put down his cutlery and pushed away his half-eaten breakfast, then got up and left quickly.

* * *

"And what are you doing, Cobb?" asked May, pausing in the doorway of the dormitory. Jim was standing by his bunk, unpacking his daybag with his back to the man.

When he said nothing, May stepped into the room and stopped five yards behind him.

Jim turned and looked at him, knowing it must have looked like dangerously insubordinate indifference when he went back to what he was doing.

"Cobb, you'll answer when I ask a question," May said.

But Jim continued to unpack his bag without saying a word.

97

May was suddenly furious. "Where in the world do you think you are?"

Jim stopped without turning around. Head down, he said, "Sir, we can't pretend it didn't happen. Frank was one of us."

"Pretend?" May's face contorted as if he'd heard something incredibly stupid. "Pretend? Is that what you think's happening?"

Jim was poised for a rearward attack.

May said, "Right now, pretending is exactly what some of us are going to do, including you, Cobb."

Jim turned his head slightly in disgust. Quietly inflamed, he continued to unpack his daybag.

"Cobb, this is the United States Navy, for Christ's sake. We fight wars. It's a terrible thing, but colleagues are going to die. I can promise you—"

"I know that, sir. But to just carry on with no regard for a fallen comrade is downright disrespectful—"

"Cobb, we honor and mourn our losses in an appropriate and timely manner, but that doesn't mean we stop when something important needs to be done. We are preparing to fight for our country." When Jim didn't respond, he continued. "What about our other colleagues? What about the men on the Cabot today? They've prepared, haven't they? They're waiting for you, aren't they? What about all the men who spent years training you for your big moment today, Cobb? How long have you been on this?"

Jim sighed and said, "Third year, sir."

"Right. And this is it. It's your big moment to get your shit over the line. Are you going to throw it all away? For Baum? For something you had no hand in? Pull yourself together, Officer Cobb. It's a terrible thing, but it won't be the first time you or

98

the rest of us lose a colleague."

Jim felt pained and suddenly quite expendable—like Frank, he supposed. Despite his training, any one of a million dangers could take him out too. The world, May had hinted, would go on after the merest pause.

"Now, I want you to pack up again, clear your head, and ship out, Cobb. Or you'll miss the boat and your chance to fly high for the Navy. Is that what Baum would have wanted?"

May left him to follow orders. It seemed unreal that he was being encouraged to succeed for the first time, instead of being hurled out.

Jim looked at Frank's spotless bunk again and wondered who would tell the Baums what had happened if they didn't already know. He thought he should volunteer as an equal rank. He'd met them before, but he was afraid of the idea, having seen what it took for the officer and chaplain to visit him and his mama in fifty when his father had gone.

* * *

Later that afternoon, Jim flew downwind in Cabot's landing pattern over the sea. Outside the Corsair's left window, the ship's diamond Fox Flag flapped high in the wind, its vast silver-gray hull shimmering in the Gulf of Mexico.

His plane was second in line to land. The cadet in front was already straightening up for his first trap as Jim began the countdown for his own left turn just ahead. He would be ninety degrees from the landing spot on the deck, then on the home stretch after another left.

He glanced at a photo of his mama and father, hung up in the upper left corner of his instrument panel. JoAnn's was secured on the opposite side and he regretted not having one of Frank. He resolved to finish the job for them all today, knowing that they would be with him every second, no matter what happened.

With moments to go, he thought back to being shot into the air by the ship's steam catapult. There had been more cadets than planes today, so they'd lined him up until one became available. The Corsairs, usually parked in a row with their wings folded, were all taken when he'd arrived, and it hadn't helped that one of the planes had stalled over the flight deck and landed on a wingtip. Its gear caught a rail on the port catwalk, but it kept going and careened over the edge, suspending itself upside down over the water. No portable crane was available, so the pilot climbed up a tow rope while they tied the aircraft to the hull. The event had halted flight operations for over thirty minutes before they raised the flag again to resume qualifications.

He was on the starboard catwalk when his plane finally pulled up with a jubilant cadet, who high fived another as they walked away. It was chocked with the engine still running when the plane captain gave him the signal to climb aboard. Cockpit hands strapped him in, but the radio was all static. He tuned it and did a radio check with the landing signal officer, then moved up to the catapult launch position. With a nervous two-finger V, he was ready to go. The launch officer returned the gesture. He throttled the engine to full power, put the stick in neutral and tucked his elbows into his sides. Taking a deep breath, he pulled the stick back toward his groin. The catapult walloped his butt, and he passed over the end of the deck a millisecond later.

His heart stopped and he nearly turned blue as the plane immediately plunged toward the water. Thankfully, the wings found lift and he climbed away from the ship. He leveled out quickly, started breathing again, and entered the landing pattern, thinking of how close he'd come to ditching on his very first attempt.

He was now at the ninety-degree left turn and glanced out the canopy. After adjusting the throttle and fuel mixture, he put the gear down, set the flaps, and turned to port. The plane in front hit the deck and got the signal to cut its engines—but it didn't clear fast enough, and Jim's plane, right behind, got a wave-off. He slammed the throttle, climbed out again, and made a second pass, cursing softly for losing his first attempt.

The deck bounced around like a corkscrew in the choppy water on his second approach. If he flew too low or too slow, he'd plow into the ship if it hit a swell at the wrong moment. A falling vessel would mean another go-around. He came in carefully and got the cut engine signal, but hit the deck too hard and bounced up. A second wave-off followed.

Jim throttled back and climbed out again as the orange-striped, reflective-suited landing signal officer flagged *Damned Near Killed Us All* in LSO with his fluorescent paddles. Jim wondered what had just happened and realized he'd forgotten to drop his tail hook. But where was it? The Corsair was so new to him that no one had explained a deck landing in the plane. He radioed the LSO.

"It's the T-shaped handle," the man said. "You got that?"

He did. And he also got that he had already done two patterns without a single landing toward his success quota of six. His nerves flared as he turned left and downwind for a third time, easing the power to descend to one hundred feet. Eighty knots and fifteen feet above the deck, he received the blessed cut engine signal again and hit the third wire.

He pumped the air with his fist after the barrier stopped him, though it felt like slamming into an invisible wall at a hundred miles per hour. They pulled his Corsair back onto the catapult after a brief arrest.

His second trap went well, and his confidence grew with each turn. Over the next thirty minutes, he made four more landings, catching the wire each time without drama.

His legs were shaky when he finished and got off the plane. The deck officer came up and announced to the plane captain that he had completed basic training. The man turned to Jim and said, "Off you go, son."

And that was it. Jim looked around. There was no ceremony.

He stopped to calm his nerves as they pulled the plane over to clear the landing area. He had made it over the line and strutted across the deck like a new Midshipman First Class when another Corsair came in and bounced toward the bridge. The pilot immediately throttled and climbed away, narrowly missing the tower.

Jim saw the stricken plane still tied to the side of the ship when they returned to the dock. Lacking a crane, they dropped and folded it onto the pier with an almighty crunch.

* * *

Early-March 1953, Corpus Christi, Texas

Jim returned to his native Texas to complete advanced training in the World War II-era F6F Hellcat before it was retired.

In early fifty-three, he emerged from Corpus Christi's Naval Air Advanced Training Command as a brand-new ensign, receiving his hard-earned Wings of Gold from the station's commanding officer.

Eager to celebrate the day, he called his mama and told her to invite JoAnn to the ceremony. He wanted to test the idea of getting married, believing she would wait even if the Navy sent him somewhere first to collect their dividend.

His intention didn't surprise Susan when he called. She was thrilled and said she had always thought he would be good for her. But she also revealed that JoAnn hadn't been home much, so she suggested that he write to her. He said he had written, although he hadn't popped his big question—he wanted to do that in person.

"So are you going to talk to her? Don't say a word—just tell her to come for the wings," said Jim.

"I'll talk to June and see what the girl is up to. It would be good for her to get away. Oh, that would be wonderful. You could fly her around the world."

He wrote to JoAnn, and a nerve-wracking week passed without a reply.

He tore open her mail when it arrived the following week. Fortunately, she had met Susan, although she had been busy and away a lot. Nevertheless, she was immensely proud of him and said she too had news to share after such a long time.

Intrigued, he was mightily relieved and began to sharpen his pitch.

JoAnn had never looked so enchanting in her cream and bright red, rose-patterned prom dress at the wings ceremony. She'd blossomed in her three years' absence, albeit with a certain adult reserve, he thought.

Susan did the honors of pinning the precious wings to the left breast of his pristine whites, while JoAnn pointed out a spot above the pocket. And despite her reservations about the

103

whole endeavor, Susan declared that she had buried her initial misgivings. That didn't seem likely, but he would know how she really felt with news of his first assignment received that morning.

"Where will you be stationed now, Jim?" Susan asked as they walked arm in arm away from the crowd after the ceremonial hat toss. JoAnn walked at his other side, clasping a small dress bag in front with both hands.

"A new squadron in Jacksonville, Mama. Away from home, but that's okay. They just spent a million bucks qualifying me, so I was hoping they'd keep me under wraps and out of harm's way for a while." Susan hadn't guessed what he'd inferred. "So I'd better not get into a car accident or anything," he added, laughing it off unconvincingly.

"Are they going to send you to that war?" JoAnn probed. She seemed nonplussed.

"Well, an officer's life means fighting an enemy, and since there aren't any at home, it'll have to be somewhere in the world. I get one hundred forty-nine dollars—not forgetting the fifty-five cents—plus hourly flight pay. And it's a nice long trip if a plane can go that far. All I have to do is fly, and fly some more, and just keep flying." He paused for a moment to reminisce. "I can almost hear Frank counting the money."

Susan nodded. "It's a terrible thing. He didn't even finish his training. I can't imagine how his parents must have felt." She looked at him and flicked an eye at JoAnn, realizing what he'd just said. "Wait a minute, if it can go that far? Jim?" Her jaw dropped as she asked, "Are you saying ...?"

They stopped walking. "It's a Korean squadron, Mama. I'm about to be shipped off to the war." JoAnn and Susan remained silent, so he continued. "I've got a little more training in the

Shooting Star first."

They looked puzzled.

"A new jet for the Navy. Then ... I'm off." Another small silence followed as they processed the news.

Susan looked away, sighed, and said she knew it was coming. "Oh. Why else would they give you all that training?"

"There's a shortage of pilots, so there isn't the time to settle into the new role. I'm sorry, Mama. Orders flew in this morning before my wings."

JoAnn reached out and held his forearm while Susan clasped hers on his other side.

Although he was ready to propose to JoAnn, it suddenly occurred to him that he might not actually see her again if his next step ended in disaster.

CHAPTER 14 - HITCHED

Same evening

The sky was calm and rarely overcast as Jim and JoAnn walked along the newly opened one-and-a-half mile Corpus Christi promenade that evening. Susan had already left for home. They strolled past wooden benches overlooking the ocean to a small white pavilion next to a seaside cafe. Jim devoured an ice cream cone, trying not to get it on his uniform.

He talked about his jet conversion training, how he would get to Korea, and his duties while there. JoAnn warmed up slowly and said she'd forgotten there was a war on until Susan had mentioned it. To him, it sounded a little dismissive. She asked who was winning. He said he'd find out soon enough.

They entered the shelter and looked out at the ocean. JoAnn was leaning against a low side wall facing him, her dress fluttering gently in the ocean breeze. "I like your nice brown shoes," she remarked. "Very smart. And quite a shine. I could almost wear makeup in them."

"Well, they took almost three years to polish," he joked. "That's the most important lesson I've learned so far in the Navy, and maybe the only thing I'll still do when I'm eighty," he said. "It's a precision craft, and it's brown with everything but the blues. Although I'll never forget the day I wore black to my first uniform inspection. The commanding officer was not pleased. I got duties for a week."

JoAnn said she had almost finished studying journalism and was focusing her efforts on civil liberties for women and underrepresented groups. He wasn't quite sure what that was, but her choice didn't surprise him. She'd mentioned something like that before. She lit up and said it took her away from home to see the impact on ordinary people, and she relished the idea of righting the wrongs of the world. "I understood nothing when I was young. But the problems were hidden in plain sight everywhere."

"Oh, but you did, JoAnn. You used to tell me things and I just listened. I can't promise I remember everything," he said jokingly. "Things were simpler for us back then anyway."

They talked about old times and growing up.

Not wanting to be obvious, but to sound her out, he asked sheepishly and with a grin, "Well, speaking of the good old days, how's your family?" He looked at her and pushed the boat out. "Maybe I should go see them again if I get a chance when I get back. It's been such a long time, and you know ... we could talk about the future."

As innocuous as the words were, JoAnn immediately knew where he was going. There could only be one reason for visiting her parents. She hesitated at first. "Now's not a good time." It was assertive, and she surprised herself.

Jim's grin faded. "Everything okay?"

JoAnn grew frosty. "Yeah, they're fine ... just, I don't know when I'll be home, and you probably won't have time."

"Sounds like you've moved out."

"Well, no. I'm just trying to get on the ladder, you know.

Meeting people." She was quite matter-of-fact.

He stopped, knowing something was up. "Did you get my letters?"

"Yes." She seemed unwilling to say more.

"Is something wrong, JoAnn?"

"No." She shrugged subtly, not looking at him. "You stopped writing. I guess you were busy."

"I did?" He didn't think he did. "Well, okay, maybe when we started flying, things slipped a little. I was on the hamster wheel twice a day."

She just nodded.

"And before that, I wrote. Remember when I passed my exams? My carrier qualification? That was scary."

She looked straight at him, her cogs clearly turning.

"What?" he asked.

"I didn't get them."

"You know, yours stopped too," he said, softly. He felt more mystified than ever.

Confused, JoAnn turned to the vast expanse of sea.

Jim said awkwardly, "It's great you nearly finished college. I'll be gone, but not for long."

She didn't answer.

He sidled up and asked, "What is it? You're not telling me something."

She looked at him, then back out to sea and said, "Jim, it's not you. With a deep sigh, she added, "I have something to tell you." She rubbed a tear from her left eye.

"Did I say something? What did I say?" he asked, sensing that everything was about to go horribly wrong. Trying not to invoke a demon, he said, "Okay, I'm sorry, I didn't mean to ... I just thought ... I realized what I needed when we were apart."

She reached up and put her slender fingers on his lips to stop the words. She'd done that before. Except, this time it felt different. He saw through the yawning silence that she didn't feel the same way about him.

She wiped away another tear, and said, "I'm so sorry. I thought you were gone."

"Sorry for what?"

"I'm engaged."

Jim felt like the enemy had just thrown a grenade at him.

After another pause, JoAnn said, "I'm getting married, Jim." He was stunned. She looked shaken.

He broke the silence. "Married? You didn't say anything."

She could barely look at him. "I'm sorry. I had to leave home. You know I couldn't stay there."

"But that doesn't sound like ... Who is he?"

"He's a professor from college ... my professor."

Jim swallowed hard. "Well, JoAnn, I ... I should congratulate you. That's wonderful news."

She dried her face and perked up a little. "He's a social scientist and a journalist, and I'm thrilled about that."

After another silence, he said, "I hope you'll be happy," but it was sterile and unconvincing. He gave her a tentative hug, still dazed by the news.

She dug into her purse and pulled out a white envelope. "I want to give you something."

He looked down at it.

"I want you to keep this and open it if you ever find yourself alone and in trouble out there."

He took the envelope. "What is it?"

"It's just something I want you to have. Promise me you'll keep it with you." She held his gaze. "I understood why you

109

had to leave. But I wished you hadn't."

"JoAnn, I'm so sorry. Why didn't you say?"

"I didn't want to get in your way. It was what you wanted when your father didn't come back."

He scanned the envelope looking for a corner to peel, but she held his hand. "How will I know when to open it?"

She put her hand over his heart. "You'll know."

Clumsy banter filled awkward silences as he drove her back to the station. His head spun as her bus pulled away, thinking that he may never see her again. He drew the envelope from a back pocket and looked at it again, wondering if it was really over. Was their life together finally done? He'd gotten his wings, and for three years it had been his only goal. Now, as a Navy jock and officer in crisp whites, he had expected to feel like the envy of the world in his moment of triumph. But she'd outgrown him, and he'd been so out of the picture, he hadn't even known it. How could he have been so naive? All that remained now was the warpath he alone had chosen.

A car barreled up the boulevard, honking loudly and interrupting his thoughts. A passenger in the back shouted cheers, while another in the front held a celebratory red torch out the window. It was a set of new ensigns.

All Jim could muster was a bearish LSO wave-off.

CHAPTER 15 - PANTHER

March 1953, Korea

Jim felt the full weight of his decision to join the Navy when he crossed the Panama Canal aboard the USS Leyte a week later. He would join Carrier Task Force 77 off the coast of Korea. Even though he was still a Navy nugget, they were shipping him off to war to take bullets for people he knew nothing about. The enemy could kill him like the countless pilots before him. That explained the shortage. It occurred to him over and over that if he'd just stayed closer to home for a simpler life, like his mama had said, he'd probably still have JoAnn with him. Now, there was nothing he could do. He'd just have to survive it one mission at a time and hope to God he came back without a lifelong injury for a souvenir.

He tried to gee himself up by thinking it was his moment to get back at the Communists for killing his father, though he couldn't shake the dread that he might befall the same fate.

Fortunately, he shed most of his nagging fears over time, even though he made two death runs over enemy territory every day. After four months of service and fifty-two missions in the Navy's Corsair, he remained alive and unharmed. He was surprised at how quickly it had all become routine, like simply driving a cab to work every day. And after a while, it didn't seem so bad—he'd return to a hot shower, change into his slacks, and join the boys for dinner and the ship's jawbreaker stuffing contest—though his upper lip wasn't quite long enough to clamp the clincher. He was the fastest to drink thirty-two ounces of milk without throwing up. A movie usually preceded bedtime each day. He thought about JoAnn and started a letter, but hadn't finished it.

The Navy transferred his squadron, VF-51, from Carrier Air Group 11 to the Essex and assigned him to take delivery of the Navy's first combat ready jet. The F9F Panther was a straight-winged fighter with four twenty-millimeter cannons, a pair of five-hundred-pound bombs and six high-velocity rockets. Seeing it suddenly rekindled his fear of death.

As one of the few pilots to complete jet conversion training during his final weeks at Jacksonville, he knew it was slow and couldn't climb as fast as the new Soviet MiG-15 he'd encountered several times in the northern part of the war zone near the Manchurian border. It also couldn't turn as fast with all its ammunition, so it was no match in a dogfight. The Navy had no tactical air-to-air maneuvers for the plane when it arrived, and it stalled unannounced on landing. It looked like it might kill him first if the enemy didn't.

He'd barely finished reading the Panther's flight manual when he was called up for his first mission inside the death trap. He and his wingmen would be carrying napalm to drop on the North Koreans and the Chinese fighting alongside them.

The Navy parked a supply ship against the Essex for a second time one week in July fifty-three. He saw food and other supplies being transferred on high ropes between the ships as he walked to the ready room that afternoon for the second launch briefing of the day. But all he could think about was shore leave in Yokohama. Maybe his father had been there.

"Sixty bucks for six days," his buddy said, as they walked together.

"Sounds like a bargain when you put it like that. Frank would have loved it."

"You need to head for the pleasure quarters. A pan-pan, a roof, and all the beer you could want for only sixty bucks. I'm telling you, it's the best thing our government ever sponsored."

"Talking deals, do you think they'll get one?"

"I sure hope so. We'll all be home for Christmas," his buddy said, jokingly. "Where did you hear that?" They turned a corner and entered the room. "But I still don't understand why we're getting shot at when a deal's so close."

"The Chinese and North Koreans are pushing south to get the best terms," the XO said, overhearing them.

Jim and his buddy sat in the fourth row behind a dozen pilots as the officer turned to a war map on the mission board.

"We'll be working the railroads this afternoon," the XO said, pointing to the location with a stick. "Segment Delta-Tango. The Reds are stockpiling supplies beyond mortar range, north of the main line of resistance. This afternoon we'll hit a pair of trains that are supplying the enemy with food, medicine, and weapons at the war front. The trains are on a mountain pass, possibly hidden in a tunnel by the time we reach the objective. If that's the case, we lock them in the hole. The return route is south, then east, taking out targets of opportunity."

Jim saw the main line of resistance on the map. It followed the thirty-eighth parallel across the peninsula and two hundred miles south of the target.

"Radar has the trains north of the Pyongyang Iron Triangle,

near Songchon. They could be at the front in twenty-four hours. But they're moving supplies at night to stay under cover. So the trains have to be taken out before nightfall tonight."

The XO and the pilots glanced at a series of aerial reconnaissance photos pinned to the board.

"So, back to the question. Why? At this point?" asked Jim's buddy. "Why not just wait and see what happens? Why put more men in harm's way?"

"We have to squeeze them for everything we can before a deal. Every last drop before agreeing to a ceasefire. They have to know that we will not back down, that life will get worse if they wait any longer or capitulate. They think the Americans are finished, but they have to believe that two years of stalemate will turn into four, eight, ten. We must bring their ink pens to the table, gentlemen."

"But that's so close to MiG Alley. We know the Panther's no good at interception," said another pilot.

"We'll do the job, then get our asses home. The Air Force will be up there too."

A quiet murmur followed as they absorbed the challenge.

The XO turned his pointer back to the aerial view. "The areas here, here, and here are littered with twenty to thirty fifty-seven millimeter radar-guided anti-aircraft guns. They shoot big-bore TNT flak. They time some to blow at altitude."

The mission had all the appeal of stomping barefoot on a hornet's nest. "A hit in this location would make it impossible to get back to base," Jim said.

"Korean Bay, west of the target, is your best escape route," said Powell, the ship's new commanding officer. He'd poked his head around the door quietly, looking for someone. "Good luck, and keep each other's wings. See you at the movies later."

Everyone looked up and acknowledged him before he was gone again.

Jim prayed he'd live to see *Yoke* for the first time, and hopefully see peace in the world as he hitched a ride up the flight deck elevator to his plane. The refueling ship, sailing on Essex's port side, had pulled away and the crisscross Fox Flag was flying again. He grumbled, sweltering in his poopy suit in the monsoon heat, and asked the deckhands to load extra rounds into his cannons, knowing that one well-executed enemy shot would bring him down like a kite which had lost its wind.

He sauntered up the catwalk, jumped into a Panther, and unfolded its wings. They positioned him on the catapult. The engine gave a great roar, and the plane ducked as the launch officer dropped his flag.

The cat yanked the plane off the front of the ship and he was gone.

CHAPTER 16 - BOGEYS

Moments later

Jim's airspeed rose more slowly than on the props, but he soon pulled up his gear and flaps and assembled with the section of six Panthers that soared skyward around him.

Aside from the necessities, there was little banter to prevent enemy eavesdropping. Everything was quiet, except for the hum of the engines. He felt a familiar loneliness that appeared whenever he flew into danger inside his little cocoon.

The section headed west over the Sea of Japan. Within twenty minutes they were over the east coast and just south of the thirty-eighth parallel. Small boats maneuvered along the brown coastline, dotted with small islands of varying sizes. The sky remained clear of rain as the section spread out, firing bursts of gunfire into the air to check their ammunition.

"Flight Control, Eagle Leader. Dry feet."

They were over land. Jim glanced down at the map sections on the flight board strapped to his right knee and saw that the route would take them over jungle-covered mountains, intersected by the occasional muddy river.

"Eagle flight, vector starboard zero one zero, report level at angels two zero."

They turned north at twenty thousand feet over Pyongyang and headed straight for their target, about a hundred miles inland.

"Eagle Leader, this is Blue. Level angels two zero, steady on zero one zero," Jim said. The section confirmed.

They were within ten miles of the target, just forty minutes after leaving the Essex. The railroad itself was now visible, winding north through valleys and canyons between four thousand foot mountains. At five miles, they turned northeast and descended again to follow the tracks.

"Flight Control, Eagle Leader here, target acquired. Between those two mountains. Two trains moving fast, heading south towards the tunnel. We have them."

"I swear I've killed this piece of track before," said one of the section. "But it looks as good as new. How'd they do that?"

"Eagle Leader. I'll block the tunnel entrance before they can hide inside. Orange and White: Flak suppression and napalm to clear the area first. Blue, you're up front on the loco."

That order was for Jim. He ran through his munitions checklist and armed his bombs.

"Green and Brown, you're on the second train."

Jim readied his combat systems. The section split. Orange and White began their dive on the target, spraying their cannons at the rail line, then dropping napalm pods into the surrounding foliage.

The remaining four planes broke off on either side and came around as violent balls of fire and smoke rose into the air. The four dived to four thousand feet and rejoined the bombing run just three miles from the target. Swirls of fog enveloped the pine mountains and hid the narrow valleys below. They threaded and skimmed their way through the contours, then rounded a corner

117

to see a storm of super-bright white and orange tracer streams erupting like lightning from the valley floor and mountain slopes. Jim's adrenaline went through the roof as small black explosions peppered the sky directly in front of Eagle Leader.

The flak quickly intensified to a new level Jim had never seen before, arching over the valley and forming a woven canopy over the misty canyons below. If he was shot down now, he'd be gone forever.

The infamous anti-aircraft radar guns fired automatically as they rounded another mountain. The enemy rushed to uncover camouflaged flak guns on flatbed trucks as others began firing into the air.

The section leader dropped to three thousand feet and pointed his nose straight at the mouth of the tunnel, now in plain sight. Jim followed.

The first five-hundred-pound bomb blew the entrance to the tunnel as the train raced to hide inside; the explosion was so powerful that it came out the other end of the hole. A handful of the enemy staggered out, screaming and clutching their ears in agony. Eagle Leader pulled up sharply to avoid the shrapnel that was already flying through the air.

Jim came up behind and dropped his five-hundred-pounder on the slowing locomotive, which screeched to a halt just fifty yards from the blasted tunnel entrance.

"Bingo!" he said, swerving to avoid the massive cloud of steam that shot up into the air, splattering the belly of his plane and its windshield as the locomotive came to a halt just twenty yards from the destroyed tunnel entrance.

Hundreds of pounds lighter, he began a steep pull-out, followed by Eagle Leader in a long, wide circle. He felt the jolt of a shockwave as Green and Brown blasted the second train just behind him. It went up like a gas station, the explosion probably visible on the main line of resistance a hundred miles south. Orange and White strafed the area and napalmed the southern section of track.

He and the leader dived to five hundred feet for a return strafing run behind the first two planes, but the flak continued to increase with huge shooting streamers that lit up the sky like a dozen firework plants had just gone up together.

He said a quick prayer, then hurtled down to fifty feet like a roller coaster, almost touching the treetops as he swerved to avoid enemy fire. The second train had slammed into the back of the first, and more than a dozen cars had derailed, littering the trackside just short of the tunnel entrance. Enemy troops in khakis with ammunition belts across their torsos were already on their backs, spraying bullets at anything that moved in the air.

He came in and fired his guns. The deafening noise filled the plane, along with the smell of spent cordite, with each round exploding like grenades on the ground.

A group of what appeared to be unarmed civilians or prisoners fled the scene on oxcarts, and with wooden racks hoisting belongings on their backs. Jim let go of the trigger. One of the enemy kneeled down, pulled a rifle from the cart, and took aim. Jim hurriedly armed a missile as the man fired a few rounds, then jumped sideways and hurtled down a slope into the tree cover. A shot hit Jim's plane as his rocket hit the ground, though it missed the enemy.

Except for a few radio-controlled guns, the flak quickly subsided as they raced away from the target area.

"Okay, Eagle Flight, balls to the walls. It's curtains for this show. Head for the barn before The Lord changes his mind."

The group reassembled at fifteen thousand feet and flew a wide circle north toward the Sea of Japan. A visual damage check of the aircraft revealed nothing out of the ordinary: wide gashes from ground gunfire and flying debris, splattered mud and organic matter, possibly bits of human flesh and blood that the poor deckhands would have to clean.

"What's on at the movies tonight?" Orange asked.

"Wiley Coyote, of course," Red said.

Almost immediately, Jim saw a silver glint in the sky to his left. In the distance, white vapor trails crossed the clear sky. "Leader, this is Blue," Jim said. "Do you see any contrails? Twelve o'clock. Friend or foe?"

"Looks like an Able Dog. Probably from the Rusty Bucket."

"There's three, maybe four."

The leader squawked the Navy Able Dog, but got no response. He squawked again, to no answer.

Suddenly the tension was palpable in every word. "Eagle Flight, come port zero two zero. Incoming bogeys should be at your twelve o'clock, heading south at around four hundred knots. High."

Jim saw that this was no section of Able Dogs. As he turned, several shiny swept-wing MiG-15s passed at around twenty thousand feet.

"Eagle Leader, this is Blue, tally-ho, four Bandit locos in the air. Chinese? Korean?"

"They look like flying blowtorches," White said. "But that's an AD out there. They're on to him."

An unfamiliar voice appeared on the comms. It was the pilot of the Able Dog on their frequency. "Lieutenant Chuck Moore, Valley Forge. I need some help. I brought you five bogeys from MiG Alley. Sorry fellas."

"Are you alone?" asked Eagle Leader.

"My wingman's been downed further north," said Moore.

"I see only four," Jim said. He scanned the sky furiously for impending doom. "Did you say five?"

Suddenly, out of nowhere, orange tracers flew across the sky as something hit his plane from above, striking like gravel on a tin can. Four MiGs dived and split for an attack, quickly surrounding the Panthers.

Jim rolled after them, but his plane was struggling to keep up, just as he'd feared all along.

Two MiGs turned and shot overhead with a deafening roar, and for a moment, he lost all sense of where he was in the air. He concentrated on his instruments and turned again with a burst of fire from his cannons. Still disoriented, he climbed to stay above them.

His tail was clear as he followed a MiG. He rolled over a ridge in the air and sprayed his guns. The MiG simply turned on a dime, and as Jim followed, one of his wings stalled, and he tumbled through the air toward Earth. He quickly regained lift and the plane straightened. Damn it, he thought, I'll know better than to do that again.

Another MiG shot forward, firing on all guns.

Jim pulled hard left as Flight Leader came up behind him and blasted its tail. Left and right, a horde of aircraft twisted, turned, and fell through the sky like a swarm of wasps. Two Panthers shot forward as a MiG plummeted to Earth with a trail of smoke. Another plane, chasing another Panther, nearly harpooned the pilot as he bailed out.

"Go left! Left!" Jim yelled over the thunderous roar of his engine. He caught another MiG chasing the Able Dog just as three tracer streams shot past his canopy. Two MiGs had broken formation and were chasing him, targeting his tail. Jim swerved in the air, but the MiGs just kept coming.

Another Panther appeared and fired behind them. The MiGs broke off and swerved left and right. Several new tracers, aimed at the friendly Able Dog, shot across the sky. Jim responded with another burst of gunfire, but they got away again.

Suddenly, out of nowhere, a fourth MiG appeared on Jim's tail, its guns blazing.

"Eagle leader, one on my six. I can't shake it!" he said into his microphone, calling for help.

"I'm on it," Red said. "Okay, dive buddy, dive!"

Jim pulled a stall turn and brought the plane to a near stop in the air before it dropped like a stone from the sky. He hit the left rudder hard on the way down and pushed the stick to full opposite lock as he stared vertically at the ground below, thinking the wings were about to be blown off. They regained lift and the plane straightened with the ominous sound of wind rushing over creaking metal. He would have puked over such a fancy move in his training days.

He hit the throttle again and got a deafening roar, but cursed the jet for its slow response. Finally, it gave a smooth release of power that threw him backward into his seat with a surge.

The plane rose again, but his relief was short-lived as two MiGs closed in again.

He faced them and fired another deafening blast from his guns. The shots hit the left MiG, causing it to wobble sideways and nearly knocking out his wingman. The remaining MiG fired its guns back at him, peppering his right wing with a new set of holes.

The sky was filled with orange tracers chasing spinning planes. He couldn't see who was who.

Jim instinctively ducked as if someone had thrown something at him. He felt a trickle on his cheek. There was blood on his face—not a gush, but just enough to cause a mild panic. A splinter had struck him from somewhere. After a momentary wobble, he prayed there wasn't something more fatal that he hadn't noticed. He wiped the small wound and looked over his entire body, relieved to see that there were no holes or missing parts, nor any torrents pouring out of a larger breach. He looked up again, determined not to be outgunned, when two more MiGs appeared out of nowhere and closed in. In sheer terror, he realized they had trapped him.

He zigzagged, as tracers shot across the sky, and volleyed shot after shot back at the MiGs, though he barely held them off. The closest MiG swerved to avoid them. Strangely, as it got closer, he saw the face of the enemy with a red silk scarf around his neck.

Then they turned and were gone.

He scanned the empty sky for whatever malevolence was lurking out there and about to shoot his ass off, feeling certain that he could not have escaped the fight.

A deafening bolt of silvery yellow shot through the air directly above him, almost hitting him. He checked his six again, then fired his cannons at whatever he could, immediately recalling his flight instructor's advice precisely not to do that.

He looked up again and saw a white star on the belly of the silver beast, instantly recognizing it as an Air Force F-86. Another one shot over the top. A third came up on his tail. The American jocks had piled into the fray and pulled away two MiGs. Within moments, the surrounding skies had quietened, and other Panthers had straightened up too.

The split-second relief was short-lived, as the third MiG fired at him. Its bullets missed by what felt like inches as Jim turned. It shot past in pursuit of the Able Dog, and he saw that it was the pilot with the red silk scarf again.

"He's on my six. On my six," Moore yelled from the Able Dog.

Jim turned to follow the MiG and fired, determined to prevent another escape.

"Okay, turn left! LEFT!" he ordered Moore.

Jim lined up the MiG in his sight and fired another burst into its belly, then broke sharply right and dived deep into the mountains to draw the MiG away from the Able Dog.

The MiG turned right. He heard a bang as sparks shot out of its engine. They both tumbled to the ground, with Jim a hair's breadth ahead.

But he wasn't fast enough on the turn. The debris smashed into his windshield, drawing a large, ominous crack in the glass right in front of him.

A flame appeared from the MiG as it spiraled steeply in a smoking trail, its guns blazing at him in its last, desperate moment.

Jim lost control, barely gripping the stick of his plummeting plane with his flailing hands. The earth's horizon spun around in his eyeballs like a pair of Catherine wheels. He swung forward in his harness, his nose almost touching the instrument panel. His right cheek stung again. He raised a trembling hand. Fresh blood oozed from the wound as it rushed into his head with great force, dripping into sheets of diluted sweat as he hurtled toward the ground. He was sure he must have used a gallon of water in the last ten minutes alone. The plane sped up, and he could see the mountains and valleys, flak guns, and enemy soldiers standing wide-eyed and paralyzed in front of him as he careened straight toward them.

He was going to crash at any moment unless some miracle saved him. Suddenly it looked like the game was up. Groping around for his air brake and pulling hard on the stick, he expected to die within the next thirty seconds.

CHAPTER 17 - CABLE

Moments later

Flak tracers from the ground lit up the sky again as the engine screamed, lifting the nose five hundred feet from Jim's complete termination.

Disbelieving what had just happened, he caught his breath and leveled off. Barely fifty feet above the trees, he looked around for the rest of his section while searching for a way out of the mountains.

"Eagle Leader, this is Blue. Seeing red. Heading wet-feet."

Just when things couldn't get any worse, Jim heard a deafening clunk, as if a giant finger had jammed itself into the right wing. The Panther staggered sideways. The force knocked off his goggles. He couldn't believe it. Was he hit again? By what? Furious, he looked around, but the Chinese MiGs from the dogfight had gone somewhere he no longer cared about. The flak had died down too. The folly of his move suddenly hit him as a second sickening thud pounded the plane. The tank on his right wing tip was gone. A high-tension cable strung across the valley by the enemy had whipped around and wiped out his antennas, pitot tube, and a chunk of the rudder. Suddenly, he realized he'd flown right into the wire trap and yanked the entire thing from the ground.

He grabbed the stick and climbed quickly, knowing there was no earthly way out of this morass if he lost the plane now. Fortunately, the shortened right wing hadn't stalled or caused an uncontrollable roll.

But where was everyone? His eye caught the section a few thousand feet above and a few miles to the right. The MiGs were gone, presumably heading north, probably chased home or shot out of the sky by the Air Force F-86s.

"Eagle Leader, this is Blue again. I'm hit. Heading wet-feet. Do you copy?"

"Blue, Eagle Leader. Korean Bay's closed. Bogeys. Advise heading south. Land over the bomb line. Continue south."

Jim looked at his long-forgotten lap map and wiped the blood and sweat from his wound. He turned the plane toward Incheon, knowing it was the shortest route to the main line of resistance, where he'd hopefully find the bomb line. A friendly ocean lay just beyond the MLR.

He cleared the highest mountains, but found that his plane had no climb left. He coaxed it on and fled south, looking for a place to ditch if necessary. But the landscape was nothing but wooded mountains. And it was getting dark. This plane couldn't fly at night. He pulled out a flashlight, checked the hydraulic pressure gauge, and saw it hovering near zero.

"Blue, you're streaming gas."

Great, he thought. A vapor trail would now identify him to the enemy.

"Blue, this is Red. I'll fly wing with you. We'll get you over the MLR."

"Too late. I'm losing RPMs. And the sun's going down. You boys head home if you're done, or you'll have to spend the night

127

with me … and some enemy … and a war movie … very life-like, though."

"Bail out and we'll come get you."

"Too low. I'll have to land—or ditch, if I can get this thing over water. I didn't drink nearly enough in Pensacola."

The section followed Jim for another ten minutes until his fuel warning came on. "Bingo minus one," he said, seeing only fifty gallons left.

He extended the landing gear and heard the wheel doors open. The tires were just barely out and he got an unsafe indicator. Unable to land on them, he jettisoned his rockets, making sure there were no dwellings; his instructor would have been mad about that.

He thought hard. Landing with the wheels up in a mountainous forest seemed like suicide. He could eject and wait for a helicopter to pick him up if he survived the low altitude. But now there was no chance of getting back to a safe height of six thousand feet.

He searched again for the bomb line, almost willing to see a big white east-west line painted across the mountains.

In desperation, he pulled the pin on the carbon dioxide bottle, which blew the gear down.

"Eagle Leader, this is Blue. I'm ditching. I'm not counting the bullet holes in this one. See you at home. Hold my seat at the movies."

"Blue, copy. We see you. Help is on the way. We got to get home before the sun goes down."

Jim saw a flat spot ahead and thought it looked as bad a place to land as any.

At about ninety-five knots airspeed, he cut the power and set the flaps, which dropped him into the mountains. It suddenly felt dark and cold as the peak to his west obscured the fading light.

Sweating profusely in his poopy suit, he slid the canopy back over its tracks and, to his overwhelming relief, an instant coolness washed over him, as if someone had wrapped a cold wet towel around his collar on a sweltering hot day.

He turned to see small flames shooting from the belly of the plane. The engine had taken a beating.

"Great! Like a flare in the sky," he grumbled, just as his cap blew off his head in the jet stream.

Another loud bang cut through his thoughts like an axe as his left wing clipped a treetop on a mountain ridge. It felt like a shockingly familiar experience from his youth in the old crop duster, reminding him to tighten his harness before he hit the ground hard.

He pulled on the stick to flare the plane just before it dropped. It hit a rock, blowing out a half-extended tire in a cloud of dust. The gear collapsed as it scraped across the dirt, like he'd landed on compacted concrete strewn with boulders.

The plane bounced violently and slid down a hill, then jumped a lip into a swollen river like a flat rock tossed from the water's edge. It landed in the middle and began to sink immediately.

Jim fumbled to unbuckle his harness as water poured into the cockpit like it was a cheese grater. He put on his Mae West, inflated it, and looked for the shore, but it was dark and he couldn't tell one bank from the other. The monsoon water looked like a river of chocolate. The plane would be gone in a minute, carried by the current. Which way to go, he wondered, scanning the water for crocs as the plane continued to sink beneath him. Convincing himself that they couldn't survive the

Korean winters while waiting for the summers, he jumped into the water and kicked wildly toward the nearest shore, stopping mid-stroke and turning back to the plane for his radio. But the Panther's nose sunk under the water with the equipment still inside.

He swam to a muddy riverbank and scanned the undergrowth for nasties as his workhorse's tail finally disappeared under a cloud of bubbles. The engine steamed with its final hot gasp of air.

Damn it, he thought—the torches were gone too. He looked around at the strange silence around him, but fortunately no one was shooting. A flood of questions hit him instead. Where was he? Had he made it across the bomb line? If not, would he prefer to die by friendly fire or the enemy's? How would they find him with the plane under water? Was the enemy scrambling toward him? They must have seen him fall from the sky. Maybe the war had finally ended with a deal. Hooray for silence. But some luck, he thought. They must be out there somewhere. Which way now?

He sat on his butt and pulled out his soaking wet .38mm revolver, not trusting that it would actually work now if he needed it. But where was the compass? "Oh, the compass!" he fumed, throwing his hands in the air and looking longingly at the brown water.

You must know where you are; you must have a means of setting and maintaining a course; you must have a map of the area; and you must have a source of food, fuel, and shelter. He remembered the Eglin prep and suddenly felt he hadn't learned a thing at the reservation. White would be furious at his woeful unpreparedness.

With a deep sigh, he looked at a map from his kneeboard,

although he hadn't seen any useful landmarks in the forest he'd fallen into. With a pang of fear, he estimated that Incheon, in the friendly lower half of the country, was about sixty or seventy miles southwest. The capital, Seoul, was about fifty or sixty on a more southerly route. The west coast would be further the other way. But, with the compass gone, Communist Pyongyang could just as easily get him first before the sun was up.

He sat there with no idea where to go.

CHAPTER 18 - MILLER

Moments later

Five minutes later, he stood up and looked around. He'd landed on an elbow in a river that meandered left and right. Lacking inspiration, he picked a random direction, then ran away from the water in the dark, silently praying he wouldn't hit a minefield. The ground was muddy, and it soon became clear that heavy artillery had trampled the place. Within a minute, the artifacts of a fierce battle became clear. The hillside was littered with shredded sandbags, wires, and empty ammunition boxes. Some trees had been stripped of almost all their foliage by gunfire, while others were shredded or blown apart.

Jim ran straight toward a pine forest and weaved through the trees. He stopped to listen, certain he could hear voices fifty yards ahead. A small clearing came into view with a mass of troops, though it was too dark to tell if they were friend or foe.

He crouched down and looked around, wondering if he should scout the group or retreat quietly.

Wanting to see more, he crept closer to the clearing, choosing each step carefully. A lone soldier appeared in the shadows directly in front of him. Wearing a brown field hat, he stood like a sentinel with his back to Jim. Banter broke out in the clearing, though it was nothing Jim understood.

Now only twenty yards from the enemy, he stopped and cursed, then sidled up to a tree and looked around the trunk, estimating that there were about a hundred enemy troops ahead. Their big guns were trained on a slope to the right, and they had backed up large vehicles behind some of the gunners.

Jim looked for a way back and waited for the soldier to move away. For now, he'd need a better place to hide. He made for a larger trunk. His foot snapped a pile of twigs midway. He jumped for cover and froze. A minute later, he turned to look around the trunk.

Almost immediately, the painful blow of a blunt instrument struck his right shoulder.

He tumbled in agony and saw the enemy standing over him. The man was screaming at him with a pointed rifle.

Without thinking, Jim swung his feet at the man's ankles. He stumbled and fell onto his back. Jim delivered a swift kick to the man's loins while he was still down then lunged for the weapon.

Four hands now gripped the rifle as both men struggled to their knees to pull it free. Jim took another blow to his torso, but returned the gift with his heel. The man fell again, losing his hold on the gun. Jim scrambled to his feet, backed away, and aimed it at the man still writhing on the ground. His hands shot up as he screamed for help toward the camp.

Jim's heart stopped as bugles, whistles, and screams pierced the night just inside the clearing. Heart-stopping fear gripped him as a burst of gunfire erupted. Realizing he'd made a poor choice of direction, he saluted the famed General Oliver Smith for his inspired retreat at Chosin, spun around quickly, and dashed back through the trees as fast as he'd advanced moments before. Bullets whizzed past his head, splintering the forest.

Without looking back or taking aim as he ran, he raised the rifle behind him and fired several shots.

A huge explosion went off in the clearing with a massive fireball that illuminated a swarm of enemy soldiers like ants around a hole. A second explosion followed as a truck blew up behind the artillery. Stunned, Jim stopped and looked at the rifle, thinking he'd miraculously hit some ammo or fuel like a thunderbolt.

He raced across another thirty-yard clearing, looking back every few moments, thinking they must have seen him. He searched for a place to hide. Just as he was about to be impaled by a stray bullet, the firing stopped and a strange voice sounded from a loudspeaker, with words that could have come from a terrible dream.

"Hello, Tommy," said a friendly oriental voice, not unlike a waiter serving Jim noodles. "Come over, American officers and soldiers."

Jim felt puzzled and confused.

"You're on the wrong side. You must be very hot. Are you missing your wife?" The voice added.

He stopped and turned in disbelief. The message seemed sublime and ridiculous in the middle of a war zone. Was he delirious? Or dead? He looked down for a mortal wound.

"What?" he said, as a sudden burst of laughter bubbled up from somewhere inside his aching lungs. The words were comical like something from a carnival. He stifled it quickly, afraid they'd hear him. That waiter would have the last laugh if they caught him now.

After another uncontrolled cackle, a realization hit him. "Mind control? Oh, darn!" They could be erasing his brain with some kind of invisible radio field—he'd heard that that's what POWs suffered at the hands of the Communists. "Well, don't all run at once," he muttered, looking around and seeing no friendly troops emerging from the brush with their hands up. The Reds still had work to do on their offer.

He darted away from the forest, passing leaflets that littered the battlefield. He picked one up, though it was hard to read in the dark. It seemed to argue for communism versus democracy. He stuffed one in his pocket and walked quickly, not knowing where he was going.

Suddenly, an enemy patrol of about half a dozen men emerged from the trees one by one. They ran toward him. One of them raised an arm and pointed in his direction.

Jim ran up a hill as fast as he could, ducking several times to avoid new gunfire. The hum of aircraft was in the air. He knew it was the unmistakable drone of Able Dogs approaching from the other side of the mountain ahead. The enemy stopped running and their fingers were now pointing up. Two US warplanes swooped over the ridge and strafed the surrounding ground. The enemy scattered. Jim kept running. He felt ecstatic. Someone was going to rescue him. He waved his arms in the air, but stopped quickly, realizing that the enemy could spot him just as easily. He ran up the slope again until he was completely out of breath.

Two more Able Dogs fired overhead, dropping bombs on a clump of trees where the enemy was hiding. Jim covered his ears from the deafening blasts and dropped to his knees. He spotted a foxhole to his right and pounced inside.

He waited, ears covered, not daring to look out. Then, there was silence until a harsh voice said, "Here! Over here!"

Jim was astonished. It was an American voice, somewhere in the darkness outside the hole and not ten yards away. The man was laughing and moaning in pain and cried out indignantly, "Come on! What are you waiting for?"

Jim slowly raised his head, expecting it to be shot off. Another sickening groan came from the darkness. A soldier was writhing on the ground near some bushes. Jim scanned the area and made out several men scattered around the first, all completely still.

He crawled cautiously out of his hole just as the groaning man pointed a gun at him.

"American! American," Jim shouted, still on his knees. He threw his hands up into the air. "Don't shoot! Don't shoot!"

Stunned and frightened, they both froze.

"What the hell are you waiting for?" the man barked. "We got to get out of here."

Jim looked around and saw five men lying dead around him. This man was badly wounded and looked covered in dirt and blood.

"Where to?" Jim asked.

"To the bomb line, you idiot! Come on! We gotta go!"

But the man didn't get up. "Which way?" Jim pleaded.

The man pointed somewhere behind him. "That way!"

Jim saw that the man couldn't stand, so he threw him over a shoulder, grabbed the rifle from the hole, and pelted back up the hill again. He ran until he was out of breath, and just as he stopped, a shell obliterated the foxhole where he'd been hiding moments before. He saw another hole and dropped into it. This one was bigger, like a bunker dug into the hillside. He laid the man on his back against the far wall and looked around. Wooden trusses held up the roof. Someone had clearly made the hole big enough for three to four people. Empty ammunition boxes and spent cartridges littered the ground, with sandbags just outside.

Rifle fire erupted as the Able Dogs came around and strafed the enemy line again.

"Where the hell are we?" Jim asked.

With a chesty laugh, the man said, "Just like you said. We're in hell! Where do you think, asshole?"

Jim looked out carefully, but could barely see anything in the dark. He desperately wanted to get to safety. "Who are you, and where's the bomb line?"

The man threw up his hands. "Well, right here. We're in it, you idiot."

"Stop saying that!"

The man fell silent and struggled to sit up. Jim looked out again.

"And I should ask, where the hell have you been?"

Jim felt like he'd missed a date. He looked back at the man, confused.

"My company got punched in the face out there. We were waiting for you. Now they're gone. Dead! Too late! Damn you, Air Force!"

"What?"

"You were supposed to get those gooks on that hill thirty minutes ago."

"I'm not Air Force," Jim shot back, looking out again.

"Not Air Force? Who the hell are you?"

"Navy! I'm not supposed to be here."

Enraged, the man suddenly leaned forward with considerable effort, grabbing Jim's lapels with both hands. Still crouched on the floor, he yelled violently into Jim's face, "Me neither, buddy!"

He let go and fell back against the opposite wall with steadying hands on the ground.

"Just tell me which way to go, will you?" Jim said.

"What, are you blind or something? Can't you see? I can't run." The man's face contorted in anguish as he gazed down at his legs. Jim saw that the left side of his pants was shredded up to his waist and practically blackened, presumably with blood. Groaning in agony, he tried with great difficulty to shift the limb with one hand but failed.

The man leaned back, looking as if he'd expended his last ounce of energy. "Miller, Marine, 7th Infantry. We're north of the MLR," he said, panting hard. He pointed up the hill behind Jim. "That river you fell into feeds the Rimjin. You came down like a shooting star." He suddenly became angry again. "But it looks like the enemy found us before they got you."

Jim was furious with himself. He'd landed maybe a mile north of the bomb line, but still inside enemy territory. A little further south and he would have made it home. He calmed down and asked, "What happened here?"

"We were moving north to retake Pork Chop. I was part of an advance patrol that set a mousetrap to get another group of gooks out there. But where the hell was the Air Force?" he asked. "We waited and waited for the planes, then all we got was you! Landed in the water. There was no way back. They outnumbered us four to one."

"Well, it was more of a crash than a landing," Jim admitted.

"What the hell are you doing here?" Miller asked.

"Bombing run. And shooting the damn MiGs up north!" He rolled his eyes, then said, "But a wire across the valley brought me down."

Jim dropped and covered his ears as a barrage of mortar rounds fired from the forest. A sharp reply came from somewhere up the hill where the man had just pointed.

"It's about time!" Miller said, yelling over the battle. "Truman should just nuke the bastards," he lamented, panting and straining in pain. "We had them cornered, way up north."

Jim looked at him and noticed that he had a large open gash in his neck, covered in a mixture of mud and blood, and all of it oozing heavily. He moved in to inspect it when Miller suddenly lunged back at him. "Get your damn hands off me!"

Jim recoiled against the far wall.

Miller looked delirious. "I say we give them the A-bomb now. Been waiting nine goddamn months for it."

A particularly loud burst of grenade and mortar fire erupted across the valley outside. Jim looked out again as it died down. He unzipped his poopy suit and removed it from his shoulders.

"I wouldn't take that off if I were you," Miller said.

Jim stopped and looked at him.

"You might need it. You'll be sleeping out in the winter if those gooks get you."

Jim slowly zipped up and looked out again.

"You ever seen a gook? Do you fly boys even know what you're looking for?"

Jim pulled the flyer he'd found earlier from a pocket and handed it to the man.

"Oh, lucky you," he said, with obvious pleasure. "The ChiComms are good. Good! But you don't want to get caught by the gooks." He wound up again. "They don't want us here anyway. That scoundrel Rhee wants us all out," he said with a roar, leaning back and catching his breath. He cried to the sky. "What are we doing here? Just wipe the place clean and be done with it. The whole place stinks of crap anyway."

"You can't bomb crap. It sticks. Besides, we have to save the south."

CHAPTER 19 - GOOKS

A moment later

Miller sighed. "I was a reserve with a life. I'd done my time. They gave me barely a week to check my enlistment papers. There was no training, but here I was, just days later, solving someone else's problems—again."

"A retread?"

Miller was furious. "Listen, buddy! You haven't had to take a frostbitten prick out of seven inches of deep-frozen clothes for seven months in a row just to take a leak every night, have you?" He calmed down. "The cold gets into your bones. It feels like it'll never leave." He looked down at his legs again. "If I could reach my feet, I'd show you the toes I lost out here while you were taking a fancy hot shower on that boat of yours."

"I'm sorry. What did you do?"

The man paused, surprised at the question, then said, "Jazz musician." His face eased. He reached into a breast pocket with some difficulty and handed Jim a photograph. It was of his family; wife and two children. "Springfield, Missouri, if you get out of here. You like jazz?" he asked.

Jim managed a shallow smile.

"Well, I'm just going to take a little nap here," Miller muttered. "Suddenly feeling kinda tired now. It's been a busy night, as you can see."

Jim looked at him, thinking there was nothing he could do. His mind turned to his own predicament as the battle raged on outside their tiny hole. He still had no idea where to go, and without Miller's guidance he might have little chance of escaping alive. Every direction looked the same at night. By day, they might take off his head the moment he stepped outside the hole.

Miller reeled in agony and looked like he was about to drop dead. He stopped talking and lay perfectly still except for his labored breathing. Jim hoped to God he was wrong about *the bomb*.

His thoughts turned to his father as he pulled the still-shiny Douglas DC-3 lapel badge from a pocket and pinned it to his left breast. He wondered why he hadn't made time to go see JoAnn during college. Now seemed like the right time to open her envelope, but he didn't have it. He'd broken his promise.

Exhausted and out of ammunition, they both fell asleep as the battle raged on around them.

* * *

It was dawn when a rifle poked its dark muzzle against his nose inside the bunker, waking him with a start. Jim's eyes felt gritty, and his lower back and legs were stiff from sitting up all night in his drying, sweat-soaked clothes. The hole was damp and stifling in the humid morning heat. He tried to remember what had happened after dozing off that night, but flashes of lightning and the distant rumble of monsoon thunder were all he could recall. Or, maybe it was the shelling across the valley—

he couldn't tell the difference half asleep.

An American voice immediately ordered him out of the hole. He emerged into the blinding daylight with his hands in the air, and relief washed over him as he exchanged details with the unit's commanding officer. It was the 7th Infantry. They'd moved onto a place called Pork Chop, having just recaptured Old Baldy less than a mile up the hill.

They all looked battle worn, but it would please Miller to see them. Jim leaned into the bunker. "Hey, Miller?"

There was no answer.

"He's asleep," Jim said to the officer, turning back to the hole. "Miller? Look who's here."

A Marine inside popped out and shook his head. It was clear that Miller had died sometime that night.

Jim stood frozen for a moment, wide-eyed, numb, and disgusted, realizing that Miller had been right—he'd seen war for several months, but only now had he witnessed combat death up close. It was a senseless human tragedy. He was sure that the loss of a father, son, friend, and partner would be a terrible shock back home.

Jim was anxious to get to safety. He took off his poopy suit and pocketed his badge, then dropped back across the MLR as the Marines continued to advance on their precious hill.

They parked the jeep shuttle to the nearest airfield next to a cluster of enemy POWs, surrounded by a small section of waist-high barbed wire. They sat with their hands on their heads, their knees bent, and their shirts off. Large white tags hung from their necks like exhibits. With a sixth sense, Jim thought he recognized some of the captured patrol from the night's battle, and one man seemed to confirm it by looking at him anxiously for a little longer than normal.

"God picked democracy for these guys," said one of the Marines guarding them. "Hey, little Commie. Wanna see some American hospitality?" He raised his gun to hit the man in the head, but stopped short of a blow. A broad grin broke out.

"Yalu River. Yalu River. We kick your ass," the prisoner said with a wide, friendly smile.

Jim was stunned by the insolence, though the man obviously thought humor meant safety.

"Chinks learn good English, hey," the Marine said, laughing back at the man.

"Please, sir. Please, sir. Let us go. We no harm you. Let us go. Come see. We will help you. Missing your mother? Father?" It was the waiter from the night before.

The Marine swung his rifle at the head of another man seated five away. The man recoiled in agony and Jim stopped, stunned by the brutality.

"What's the matter?" the Marine said. "He's a gook. That's the way they like it. Any of you want to try some of that?" he said to the rest of the prisoners.

Horrified, Jim jumped into the jeep as it sped south through the paddy fields.

Moments later, the driver honked loudly, narrowly missing and swerving violently around a farmer's ox cart struggling to move in the knee-deep monsoon mud. A foul stench hit his nose, which he covered with his hand, thinking he might retch; though his fingers smelled little better.

The driver glanced sideways. "Chinese chow."

Jim was confused.

"You like cold, soggy rice that's been crapped on?"

"What?" said Jim, puzzled.

"The gooks crap in the fields. Fertilizer. I've been smelling their damn shit for a year now. Just don't order the curry. I guess that don't mean nothing to a fly boy like you."

Jim wondered who was fighting whom and could hardly believe the contempt for the locals on the ground.

A helo picked him up at the airfield. He was on his way to the Essex in an hour and back in his berthing compartment in three.

The first thing he did was open JoAnn's envelope.

Jim,

Take care of yourself. If you ever get into trouble with the enemy, I'll be with you to help you find your way home. Don't stop. Don't give up. Come back to me.

Love,

JoAnn

He soaked in the shower for nearly an hour, recounting the horrors of the last twelve.

After a brandy and a visit to the flight surgeon, he was cleared to rejoin the section when he returned from shore leave. They advised him to share his story with a Neil Armstrong, who had also made it back after a mountain cable brought down his plane.

The next day he was in Yokohama. First he wrote to White in Pensacola to relieve a long persistent nag. A veil had lifted in the Korean mountains. He said he owed his survival in part to the lieutenant and thanked him for torturing his indolent, immature ass over the line when he was certain to fail pre-flight.

The rest of the war was thankfully short. He flew another twenty missions, got shot at and survived, though he never again saw a MiG or a close-range enemy fighter. And the 7th Infantry abandoned its hard-fought Pork Chop when both sides signed an armistice later that month; but it was no peace treaty, and the peninsula was still at war. It seemed to turn out just as Miller had said. The UN pulled out, and Jim returned home feeling like he'd gotten back at the Reds for killing his father. He'd barely survived but wasn't sure it was enough to stop the scourge from continuing its advance across the world.

CHAPTER 20 - LOST

August 1953, Corpus Christi, Texas

Jim left the Essex in August of fifty-three and returned to shore duty at the Naval Reserve Training Center in Corpus Christi. Soon, Transport Squadron 31 had him ferrying battle-worn Panthers for the Assembly and Repair Unit too. He'd picked up several new F9F-8 Cougars from the New York factory at Bethpage to replace the Panthers that had scared him to death in Korea.

By November, he'd worked up the courage to visit Miller's family in Missouri, though he needn't have agonized over it for so long. The man's wife simply wanted to know if the military would pay for, "the sudden and unexpected loss of a husband," and demanded to know when she would get the insurance check. Jim said that wasn't his job, nor was it the purpose of his visit. She continued to read him amateur legalese from a scribbled note that he couldn't decipher anyway. And her young children hardly seemed to notice that their father had died at all. Jim didn't ask, but it seemed likely that none of them knew where in the world Miller had perished, or why.

Life went on through fifty-four. Toward the end of that year, he met Jackie at the base. A silky blonde with an incredibly bright and wide smile, she was warm, if scatterbrained, and perfectly open about wanting to bag a Navy pilot. But she had an annoying habit of shutting the bedroom door on him and talking on the phone for hours, even after he'd had a busy day at work. It all ended when she gave up her dreams of bagging a jock for a job as a personal assistant to a Miami real estate agent.

Then, in the summer of fifty-five, he met Marissa, and in fifty-six there was Barbara; both were fun while he was still figuring out what he really wanted.

All the while, he harbored an interest in the Blue Angels, the Navy aerobatics team that practiced regularly over the Coastal Bend. He abandoned the idea when they moved to Pensacola, where he'd trained.

His head had finally let go of JoAnn by the time his mama told him she'd practically moved back home with her parents. Her marriage had gotten off to a rocky start.

CHAPTER 21 - SPUTNIK

1957, Corpus Christi, Texas

In mid-fifty-seven, Jim considered his options.

Flying passenger jets seemed like a serene way to spend his post-combat years, and came with better odds of finding a partner. But he was still in his twenties, and it seemed too much like a premature resignation to a long, slow decline, simply shuttling civilians back and forth like a glorified cabbie.

He stayed put until the world changed on October fourth. The war against communism, to which he'd pledged his existence, was heating up again. A new Red threat had appeared in America's skies. The scourge was no longer confined to a distant foreign land on the other side of the globe.

It fascinated him, even as Americans struggled to marvel at the Soviet achievement of putting the first man-made object into space.

When asked about national security and what one TV reporter called the "Sputnik crisis," a worried gentleman on the news, dressed for work, said, "Someone's fallen down on the job, badly."

Another lady, shaken by the nefarious object circling out of sight above her head, lamented, "No. No, it can't be. I think we should have been the ones to have the first one. We fear they have something out there that the majority of the American people don't know about."

Because of his job, he saw a copy of a paper entitled: *A National Research Program for Space Technology,* which stated:

It is of great urgency and importance to our country both from consideration of our prestige as a nation as well as military necessity that this challenge [Sputnik] be met by an energetic program of research and development for the conquest of space.

He, like everyone else, felt a tinge of fear and national self-doubt every time he looked up at the sky.

The television networks also went ballistic, dramatizing reactions to the new threat. He watched a tightly scripted show in which an exuberant young boy tuned a radio to pick up Sputnik's signal. His cardboard uncle said out loud what virtually everyone seemed to fear.

"Just static," said the boy, scanning the airwaves with a radio receiver.

"Humans make a lot of noise, don't they? And every once in a while you can pick up the sound of the stars beaming vibrations back to Earth," his uncle said.

The boy's face lit up with joy. "Do you think aliens are talking to us?"

"Perhaps, in their strange language as they sail the oceans of space. But right now the enemy is down here. We listen to their planes in the sky, then we go get them."

"They're up there now, aren't they?" asked the boy, looking out the window at the sky. But the menace remained silent and invisible, while crickets chirped in a deceptively quiet evening.

"Do you think it has a nuclear bomb?"

"Oh, I doubt it. Putting a bomb up there would be an act of war," his uncle said.

"But we have atomic bombs, don't we?"

"Yes. We have to keep them ready for the Communist threat. But we also get our electricity from nuclear power. You heard about the new plant in Pennsylvania?"

"We talked about it at school. Are they going to build more of them?"

"Yes, and one day they'll give us limitless energy. And we'll certainly need that to get to the stars."

"That would be amazing," the boy enthused, still looking up. "Strange new worlds with ugly creatures? Do you think they're friendly?"

His uncle laughed and said, "Sure. And two heads make them extra friendly! Well, you'd better start training if you're going into space, young man." He looked back at the equipment. "Let's keep trying the radio, see if we can find that Communist threat. It's out there somewhere." He scanned the sky again. "Every ninety-two minutes. Why don't you try twenty megahertz?"

The boy twitched the radio knob a little, then stopped. "I got something," he said. He listened carefully. His eyes lit up with another twist of the dial. "I think I got it. Listen!"

The show's script played an ominous, out-of-tune, and distant beep-beep-beep that pulsed every second.

"Do you think they're going to attack? Or send information back to the Communist army? What if they strike while we're asleep?" the boy asked, glancing at the sky again.

"I think we should call the radio station and let them know, don't you?"

"Yes," the boy said with renewed urgency. "We have to warn everyone."

"Our satellites will be up there soon, too. We'll have our space back in no time. Don't you worry. Our boys are on it," his uncle assured him, looking out the window again. "We're going to start a new space agency called NASA. How do you like the sound of that?"

"Awesome," beamed the boy.

"They'll be looking for the first seven astronauts for the Mercury project soon. So we'd better start that training."

The boy dialed the radio station and said he'd heard, "Lots of beeps with war codes inside them."

Jim turned off the TV. He already knew that NASA would be born the following year.

CHAPTER 22 - TUCUMCARI

Early-1958, Southern Texas

Jim found a weekend and the energy to visit home in early fifty-eight, feeling mightily ashamed that it had taken his mama several attempts to get his attention. In truth, the old house was like a filled pothole—a reminder of JoAnn.

Susan wrote that the girl had asked about him and that she'd be home if he timed it right.

Reigning in any expectations, he detoured an old Beech-18 from Corpus to make the quick trip home. At only ten or twenty dollars—and still cheaper than a train ride or a cab—he'd pay cash for the extra fuel to avoid questions.

There was no sign of Wilman looking out the window when he turned around, as he usually did, on his mama's yard path for the first time in years. She said the FBI took him away one day during Senator McCarthy's roundup of Red suspects throughout the government. He just never came back. Jim revealed that he thought the man was definitely up to something with all his strange behavior and hiding behind curtains.

When they moved on to JoAnn, Susan said her marriage was over. The man was an abusive wanderer. Her mother, June, also looked sicker than ever after she got married and moved away.

Then one day JoAnn came home and spent a lot of time there for a married woman.

Susan said he should take her to dinner.

When Jim dropped by, June seemed pleased to see him, first checking him up and down for bullet holes. JoAnn wasn't home, but she said he could find her at the hospital where she worked as a nurse.

It was cool and clear later that evening when he went to see her, wearing his best white and blue striped shirt. He paced the corridor, wondering what to say, including why he'd come to the hospital instead of just meeting her at home.

JoAnn was shocked to see him out of the blue. He thought she looked older. She wondered if he was sick and needed a hospital bed. He said he was fine and had just come to say hello.

They went to Billy's and talked like old friends. She said she'd finished college and was working as a healthcare orderly while she found a real job in the press; caregiving was an easy trade for any girl looking to earn a crust. She'd moved back home six months earlier.

He said he picked up airplanes to repair after the war, which seemed like an eternity ago and was already largely forgotten. He was still in the Navy and not sure what was next.

Jim knew that she had left her husband. She said it had taken more than a year to work up the courage to leave; something her mother had never done with her own father. She had discovered that her father had kept from her many of the letters Jim had written while he was training before Korea; it was all a crazy attempt to keep her home.

When he asked her about her writing, she confided that journalism hadn't quite worked out either. Her husband had always preferred her as a homemaker, and she lamented that practically everyone still expected women to work in nursing anyway. She wasn't ready to fight her way into the profession alone. She still needed a male sponsor to get ahead.

Jim just listened. In the few years since their last meeting in this diner, they had faced the real world outside of school. The naive beginning had promised an unfettered adventure, but the long, thick middle had already produced real-world challenges. He hoped they'd find a graceful conclusion at the curtains.

JoAnn still wanted to get away, so he offered to teach her to fly so she could feel as free as a bird. She laughed (the first joy he'd seen in her since he could remember), then thought about it and relented, remembering that all his past promises had flown by. He saw the opening and knew he had to get her back this time.

They didn't waste a moment. It was evening when they arrived at the airfield. The breeze had picked up, though he was hot under the collar when the tops of her stockings showed as she stepped out of the cab. His heart sank at the news of bad weather, although the report showed that the storm would pass and he was good to go as long as he stayed above the clouds.

They meandered around several small jets parked for the weekend. JoAnn climbed into the Beech and leaned forward. She glanced at the instruments, wondering which seat to take. Jim came up behind her in the confined space, brushed up against her rear, and strapped her into the right seat, catching her hand as they fastened the harness.

Overlooked by a pale crescent moon, miles from home or any other visible landmark, he swung the plane around to show her what it could do, then handed her the controls, which she held perfectly straight and as stiffly as a board.

Moments later, he leaned over to put the plane on autopilot

and reached over her to unfasten her seatbelt. His right arm brushed unexpectedly against her breasts. Without warning, they grabbed each other as if making up for lost years—she by his face, inches from hers, he by the back of her head. Their lips were drawn together like magnets. His breath tasted sweet, this man she had known as a boy. His headset fell onto the instruments as he pressed his face into hers. Desperate to breathe and overwhelmed by sensation, she pushed him back and stood up, sitting astride him in his own seat and clenching hard. Clumsily and fumbling, their legs interlocked. She pressed her chest and groin into his, and their hands searched each other's bodies until they pulled apart to catch another breath. She said she'd been hoping and waiting for him to come back.

Only their will to live interrupted them when her writhing body hit the flap lever, giving the plane a sudden bounce. His face lit up with an unexpected lift that also took her breath away. He turned off the autopilot, then quickly scanned the sky and laughed, saying they'd better get back on the ground, both of them knowing what was coming next. She let go of him, straightened up, sat back in her seat, and put on her headset.

Jim landed the plane in Tucumcari, many miles from any-where. Within an hour they were in the Cactus Motor Lodge. Storm gusts rattled the windows, and a heavy rain followed in the small hours as they slept safely in each other's arms.

The next day, Jim told his boss he had to land the plane and ride out the storm.

Over the next few months, he diverted a plane he flew for work whenever he could. When it looked like the Navy was preparing to close the Corpus Assembly and Repair facility, he transferred to Advanced Training Unit B in nearby Kingsville as a navigation flight instructor.

They spent more and more time together. And their intentions and conversations turned to settling down together, which they did, getting married in the small church where they were baptized, surrounded by family and local friends.

EPILOGUE

On January 20, 1961, President John F. Kennedy delivered his inaugural address from the podium of the Capitol Building, warning of mankind's uncertain future, fourteen billion years after God created the earth in a vast and otherwise empty universe.

"The world is very different now. For man holds in his mortal hands the power to abolish all forms of human poverty ... and all forms of human life ... Let every nation know, whether it wishes us well or ill, that we shall pay any price, bear any burden, meet any hardship, support any friend, oppose any foe, in order to assure the survival and the success of liberty ... Finally, to those nations who would make themselves our adversary, we offer not a pledge but a request: that both sides begin anew the quest for peace, before the dark powers of destruction unleashed by science engulf all humanity in planned or accidental self-destruction ... Let both sides seek to invoke the wonders of science instead of its terrors ... We dare not tempt them with weakness. For only when our arms are sufficient beyond doubt can we be certain beyond doubt that they will never be employed."

The president had seen footage of Soviet ICBM launch sites, SAM nests, bomber squadrons, and nuclear submarine production lines, courtesy of his new twelve-mile-high U2 spy planes. Lieutenant Commander Cobb had seen them too, but paid with his life.

On April 12, the Soviets stunned the world again when Yuri Gagarin became the first man to conquer the heavens in the new battle for space.

Please Leave A Review

If you enjoyed *Blue Panther* as a purchased ebook, please swipe to the very end and leave a rating and review now. Just a couple of words will do.

I want to hear from you, and reviews help others discover and enjoy the book too.

You can also tap a link at 60strategies.com/BluePantherReviews or scan the QR code below.

Discover the real story!

Visit 60strategies.com/BobbyMehdwan and get the real stories behind *Blue Panther* and *Liberty One*, as well as book extracts, exclusive deals and updates! Be the first to know about the next exciting adventure.

About the Author

Bobby Mehdwan loves nothing more than writing a pulse-pounding, thought-provoking action thriller, with a heart-warming romance inside. His creative head escapes into history, the future, space, technology and Einstein's universe. He studied rocket science (honestly!) and designed military jets, so knows the territory. He also writes non-fiction professional and personal development, and is a corporate business leader by day. When he's not writing, he's probably climbing a real mountain with his family, enjoying a long bike ride or out running. Tap the links for more.

60strategies.com/BobbyMehdwan
tiktok.com/@bobbymehdwanauthor
twitter.com/bobbymehdwan
facebook.com/BobbyMehdwanAuthor

Also by Bobby Mehdwan

Read the follow on after *Blue Panther.*

LIBERTY ONE
Nukes threaten the world. International conflict propels into space. With one chance to cripple a deadly secret, will a lone astronaut survive?

60strategies.com/Liberty_One